THE EDUCATION OF CATHERINE PETERSON

KURT ROBARD

THE *Erotic* Print Society
London 2004
Printed and bound in Spain by Bookprint
S.L., Barcelona

THE *Erotic* Print Society
EPS, 1 Maddox Street
LONDON W1S 2PZ

Tel (UK only): 0871 7110 134 (order line).
Fax: +44 (0) 207736 6330
Email: eros@eroticprints.org
Web: www.eroticprints.org

© 2004 MacHo Ltd, London UK

Reprinted June 2004

ISBN : 1-898998-84-1

THE EDUCATION OF CATHERINE PETERSON

KURT ROBARD

THE *Erotic* Print Society

Foreword by Michael R. Goss

The history of erotic literature had always been clandestine, and, apart from furtive purchases of under-the-counter hardcore, American readers between the end of the war and the mid-1960s could only openly buy paperbacks with lurid covers that always promised, like first dates, far more than they actually delivered. However, the sale of two trashy paperbacks at a newsstand in New York's Times Square was to change the history of erotic publishing in the United States forever.

Previously there had been several landmark cases involving the publication of books that extended the boundaries of what was legally acceptable. These included James Joyce's *Ulysses*, D.H. Lawrence's *Lady Chatterley's Lover*, Henry Miller's *Tropic of Cancer*, John Cleland's *Memoirs of a Woman of Pleasure* and William Burrough's *Naked Lunch*. All novels which today we celebrate and study as major works of literature.

The pivotal moment came when Robert Redrup, a Times Square newsstand clerk, sold two pulp sex novels, *Lust Pool* and *Shame Agent* to plain-clothes policeman, for which he was tried and convicted in 1965. William Hamling, who published the books under his Nightstand imprint in San Diego, paid Redrup's legal bills to the Supreme Court and the resulting case, *Redrup v. New York* in May 1967, truly opened the floodgates of what was acceptable.

Hamling, and his lawyer Stanley Fleishman, firmly believed that he was not selling, as was said about his books, "commercialised obscenity," nor would he admit to "titillating the prurient interests of people with a weakness for such expression." Hamling felt his books were giving people who would never have the skills to read and enjoy *Ulysses*, *Fanny Hill* or *Naked Lunch* what they wanted.

The judge presiding over the case of Redrup, Justice Potter Stewart, went far beyond his established just-left-of-centre position on obscenity to the most radical of outlooks. Apparently the vote to affirm Ralph Ginzburg's conviction for his magazine *Eros* was his personal wake-up call. In his Ginzburg summary Stewart wrote:

Censorship reflects a society's lack of confidence in itself. It is a hallmark of an authoritarian regime. Long ago those who wrote our First Amendment charted a different course. They believed a society can be truly strong only when it is truly free. In the realm of expression they put their faith, for better or worse, in the enlightened choice of the people, free from the interference of a policeman's intrusive thumb or a judge's heavy hand. So it is that the Constitution protects coarse expression as well as refined, and vulgarity no less than elegance. A book worthless to me may convey something of value to my neighbour. In the free society to which our Constitution has committed us, it is for each to choose for himself.

Stewart's arguments were persuasive enough to convince the court to reverse Redrup's original conviction by 7-2. This decision by the United States Supreme Court affirmed that consenting adults ought to be constitutionally entitled, under the First Amendment, to acquire and read any publication that they wished, including those agreed to be obscene or pornographic, free of interference from the U.S. Government.

Under this guiding principle the Supreme Court adopted a policy of systematically reversing without further opinion ("Redruping") all obscenity convictions which reached it. Scores of obscenity rulings involving paperback sex books, girlie magazines and peep shows were overturned.

Despite an attempt to reverse the tide of pornography by new Chief Justice

Warren E. Burger in the 1970s an explosion in paperback publishing followed. Carpetbagger publishers burst into life across America, including Brandon House, Essex House, Greenleaf, Lancer, Midwood, Pendulum, Pleasure Readers, Star Distributors and many others. Every aspect of human sexuality was covered in a sexual anarchy of threesomes, foursomes and more-somes in every combination of genders and colours, often including the whole family, their pets and assorted farm animals to boot. Every genre was exploited from incest to Nazi sex with everything in-between in a total assault on the values of bourgeois culture. One can imagine publishers and authors sitting in bars coming up with titles in alcohol-and dope-fuelled brainstorming sessions which would then be commissioned out to a stable of jobbing hacks for around $500 a book.

Past Venus Press will reissue the highlights from this post-Redrup period, many of which were originally considered to have had no literary merit whatsoever and to be utterly without redeeming social importance. But that, of course, was part of their charm.

Chapter 1

In the soft light of the living room, Catherine tangled and untangled her long, gleaming legs restlessly, whilst sighs of agitation exhaled from her beautiful lips. From his seat opposite her, he watched her skirt riding higher up those legs, exposing lacy snapshots of pink flesh. His eyes darted upwards as her rapidly flaring temper left her breasts heaving and her nipples growing slowly more erect and more prominent.

"Jefferson, I wish you wouldn't be so stubborn," she finally burst out. "You know we need the money!"

Jefferson's gaze was drawn to the pretty, thin strap of her bra just showing under her loosely-buttoned shirt. He was reminded of the way her breasts shuddered at the first touch of his hands before they made love, their warmth and beauty recoiling from his cold and hungry grasp. Greedily, however, they would always then yield to his warm tongue, which circled and sucked them. As he did so, his hand would slip down between her legs and gently tease at the spirals of soft, sweet hair.

"Jefferson? Are you listening to me?"

In her anger, rising from her seat, her

nipples hard and erect, Catherine's eyes blazed with consternation at her husband's clear disinterest in the subject at hand. Striding across the living room, Catherine tossed her mane of long, thick red hair over her shoulder and continued the argument with Jefferson. For two months now she hadn't gotten anywhere with him and was determined that today she would.

"I'm tired of staying home all day and trying to balance the budget. What if something happens? What if I get pregnant? Your research grant isn't going to take care of that; we have hardly enough to live on as it is. And besides, I'm bored!"

Jefferson smiled wryly and leaned back in his easy chair, shuffling the newspaper on his knees as he attempted to turn the page. In truth, he actually enjoyed it when she got angry. Her fiery words seemed to match the colour of her red hair, and she looked extremely sexy when her hackles were up. Her green eyes flashed like emeralds, and under her shirt, her generous breasts looked as though they would almost burst through the confines. Despite her intelligence, it was often very hard to take her seriously; one could hardly ignore a body like that, even at the most desperate of times. Familiarity with it had not yet bred complacency. It was all he could do to keep himself from jumping up and stripping her clothes off, much less pay any attention to her familiar tirade.

He gazed appreciatively at her seductive form, his eyes taking in her lushly ripened breasts with their taut little nipples straining against her shirt. Her sensuality was more disconcerting than ever. The thin, slightly see-through material of her shirt allowed him to see her perfect shape, her smoothly curved abdomen tapering down to her slender waist. Her neatly flaring hips and smoothly rounded buttocks were equally well encased in her old, slightly too tight miniskirt. My God, he thought, she just doesn't realise how sexy she is! She was driving him crazy. From his low chair, her long legs seemed even longer, and his gaze slowly crawled up her slender, suntanned legs to the suggestion of her femininity underneath.

"Jefferson, you're not even listening to me," she shouted, throwing her hands up in despair and turning her back on him to return to the couch, where she curled up and covered herself with a throw. Her hurt tone and the sudden cloaking of that gorgeous body switched him back into the discussion.

"Sweetheart, I've been listening to you for weeks and you haven't changed the subject once. I don't want you to take that job at the research centre, and that's that. Look, we both sacrificed a lot to get me through my

Masters, but now that I've got the research grant, I don't want you working any more. I would've thought you'd appreciate that."

He looked at her beautiful, sullen face with its pouting lips and changed track.

"Now come on, why don't we go to the bedroom for a while and calm ourselves down?"

Catherine sighed in exasperation at her husband's soft tone of voice, knowing exactly what it meant. To him, she was simply a trophy: a sweet, sexy body with no brains. For him, her place was firmly in the home. Before their marriage she'd actually enjoyed it when he coddled her, but now it was getting on her nerves. In order to make ends meet and to support his postgraduate studies, she had got a demanding job right after college, sacrificing her own promising career as a biologist so that he could continue his. She was fed up with playing second best to his career; it wasn't fair to be treated like an idiot after all she'd done for him. And the irony of it was, he hadn't complained once when she'd worked before. It was only when the research grant had come through that he suddenly showed his true colours as a male chauvinist who wanted to dominate her and treat her with kid gloves.

The sudden change in his attitude surprised and upset her. He had no idea how much she had left behind to come here with him, and no idea how boring it was being cooped up in this small house all day, miles from town and miles from anyone they knew. The Sterlington area was a completely alien culture to her, and even the town, Fort Bridge, had little to offer. There was one cinema, a bowling alley, a lot of dingy bars and a whole lot of broken-down pickup trucks. At least Jefferson had his work: he was earning money, and at the same time he was working at his PhD thesis. What was she? Nothing but a fixture, like a beautiful piece of furniture.

Her recent unrest had started several days ago when the Centre's director, Stephen Marlingham, had offered her an administrative job. She hadn't mentioned a word of it to Jefferson, knowing how he felt about the matter. True, it was a glorified secretarial position, but there just might be a chance to move into the marine research field, and maybe she could even do something that would bring her credits toward a Masters degree. She'd told him that she would hold back her decision until she'd talked with Jefferson, but now she decided to take matters into her own hands, no matter how much her husband objected. She was sick of the way he was treating her.

"Well," she said finally, "I didn't tell you

this before, but Dr Marlingham has already offered me a job. And I've decided I'm going to accept it. I can't take any more of this life; I need to meet people, make friends and get a life. I'm bored out of my brains here."

Jefferson's languid gaze sharply switched back to focus on her face.

"Hey, what d'you mean?"

"I'm sorry, Jefferson, I know how you feel, but that's the way it's going to be. My mind's made up."

Catherine strode out of the living room, ending the conversation abruptly and leaving Jefferson in a mild state of shock.

What could he do, he asked himself? Stephen Marlingham must have cornered her at that welcoming cocktail party at his house and offered her the job on the spot. One could not refuse Marlingham. He ruled the Ellsworth-Cima Research Centre with an iron hand and had no qualms about being blunt and unpleasant when things didn't go his way. Jefferson tried to think of some diplomatic way for his wife to turn down the offer, but that would only make waves, since he knew that the director genuinely needed an administrative assistant to handle the paperwork. "Damn it," he said under his breath. For once he wanted to be the boss in the family and not have people think his wife was supporting him, but it hadn't worked out, and there was nothing he could do about it.

Nonetheless, he wished Catherine would be content with staying home and playing the role of a wife, which is what he would demand of her once he got his PhD and moved into the realms of scientific research with official credentials. If she kept on trying to assert herself the way she was now, there was eventually going to be trouble in their marriage.

Catherine returned to the room and looked worriedly at his face.

"Jefferson, are you angry?" she asked, sitting on the arm of his chair. "I meant what I said about taking the job, but I don't want to hurt you. You've got to understand my needs too."

"Oh really? Well, actually, I wish you hadn't come on so strong. I don't particularly like Marlingham, and I certainly don't like the way he cornered you at that cocktail party. He's a dirty old man, if you ask me."

Catherine had to agree, up to a point. Marlingham had seemed rather sleazy and overbearing, but this was an opportunity that she could not afford to miss. Jefferson was just letting off steam. His male ego was at stake somehow, but he would get over it. She would go mad here all day, waiting for him to come home from work. She did not want to create problems, but her current unhappiness could lead to more serious problems later and he needed to learn to be more receptive to her needs. She was also very attracted by the idea of somehow working into a position at the Centre that would give her credits toward her Masters.

She looked at the handsome, rugged face that she had fallen in love with and knew that that petulant mouth could be transformed into a wonderful smile. She had demanded enough for now, and she began to shift his angry mood to something mutually beneficial.

"Come on, Jefferson," she whispered teasingly in his ear. "I thought we were going to relax." She began flicking her tongue over his ear and running her hands through his hair, gently pulling at it. "Let's go into the bedroom. We could both use some recreation."

"Don't try to change the subject," he snorted. "You're going to do what you want no matter what I say, aren't you? For God's sake, Catherine, I don't see why you want a job – especially working in Marlingham's office. He's liable to chase you around the desk all day."

Even with his anger at a pretty high pitch, Jefferson felt himself responding automatically as his wife snaked her tongue teasingly into his ear, sending ripples of excitement through his body.

"Knock it off, damn it, you're trying to butter me up."

Catherine slid off the armrest and onto his lap, sliding one leg across his so that her skirt rose up and exposed her knickers and her scent. Fully aware of how he was responding, she dropped her hand to his lap and let it rest on the hard bulge that was already swelling inside his trousers. She felt slightly embarrassed at taking the initiative, but knew it would be the quickest and most effective way to dampen his anger.

Only once before had he been really angry with her, but once was enough. He had a tendency to entertain certain notions whilst they were making love, whispering dirty, sordid requests into her ear. They were suggestions that she found disgusting and degrading, another way in which he was trying to assert his dominance and control over her; for her part, she felt that she was managing this intimate side of their marriage very well, especially given that she was a virgin when they married. On honeymoon in the Caribbean, he had made love to her in such a gentle and beautiful way; it was everything that she had imagined and hoped sex would be. She had been willing to learn and to be enthusiastic about the new things that she'd only heard and read about before; things that were now actually happening to her.

Gradually, however, over the months of their marriage, he had become less gentle and his unusual ideas were suggested more and more often. Despite her willingness to please him, his perverted ideas changed her mood during their lovemaking, distancing him from her and leaving her almost a spectator in the act. To his credit, he had never pressed her until a certain night three weeks after they'd been married and had moved into an apartment on the University campus. That evening he had returned late from work, with a slight smell of whisky on his breath. He was carrying a pink package wrapped up with a bow, which he presented to her with a suggestive smile on his face.

"Jefferson, what is it?" she asked excitedly, taken by surprise.

"Go ahead, open it. You'll see."

Opening the box delicately, she pulled out a lacy red and black slip from the tissue paper. It was so sheer it was practically invisible. She looked at Jefferson, puzzled, and then laughed, thinking it was some sort of joke. That night, he pressed her to wear it with her high stiletto heels and she felt ridiculed and embarrassed. She grew angry, then tearful.

"How can you possibly want me to wear something like this? It looks like something a whore would wear."

"Oh, for God's sake, Catherine, don't be such a puritan. Go on, try something a bit sexy for a change."

Catherine looked at him in disgust. "I won't, I refuse!" she said, outraged, hurling the garment back in the box and locking herself in the bedroom. Jefferson hadn't even come to her to clear things up; he simply left the apartment and did not return until the early hours of the morning, when he came in drunk, his manly, handsome face exhausted and disinterested.

She felt hurt that such nonsense could cause such an argument and drive a wedge between them. She vowed not to anger him like that again, and tried to be more passionate and more expressive in the bedroom. But what was she going to do – let him take over her life completely? She had to have some independence of her own. The very thought that he wanted her to look like that, to wear that slip, still rankled with her. It would have cheapened her for the rest of her life, she was sure of that.

From that time on, there had been little cause for them to quarrel – except now. Having tasted his anger, though, she was determined to avoid a head-on confrontation and she was trying to go about things more diplomatically. And so, setting aside her inhibitions, she shifted on his lap to expose more of her panties, and continued to fondle his rapidly swelling penis beneath his pants. His angry and sullen expression was warming to her advances and his breathing began to deepen and become more rhythmic. Her hand rubbed slowly up and down the outline of his penis inside his trousers, and in response, his organ was rising to fill her entire palm.

Suddenly, unable to stand her tantalising caresses any longer, Jefferson pulled her closer to him, pushing her breasts together and up so that he could almost drown his face in their beautiful shape. He had already forgotten about her rebelliousness; in fact, he had forgotten about everything except the enticing closeness of her body.

"Come here, baby," he whispered playfully, his free hand reaching around the back of her legs and sliding slowly up the curve of her thigh.

"Ummmmh," Catherine moaned in his ear, jerking slightly from the intimate tickling sensation. She was extremely sensitive along the back of her upper thighs and Jefferson knew it. He was purposely teasing her, but still she could feel tiny goose bumps welling under his fingers. Jefferson, for his part, grinned wickedly from his sitting position and continued to play his fingers over his wife's long, naked legs, pushing his hand all the way up under her miniskirt to brush his fingers over her vaginal mound, so tightly sheathed in her silken panties. Above him, Catherine was squirming with pleasure, and her full, sensuous lips were parted in anticipation. Screw the job, he thought to himself. If she wanted a job so damn badly, she could have it. It was her delectable body that counted now. As his outstretched middle finger eased its way inside her panties, she squirmed as if to protest, but yielded to his advances.

"Baby, I'm gonna fuck you real nice," he breathed, his finger beginning to rub teasingly around the hair-lined lips of her wildly throbbing vagina beneath her panties.

"Yes, yes, Jefferson," she moaned excitedly. "I want you too." Her eyes were closed tightly shut, her hips grinding down hungrily against his, and even his foul language did not put her off this time, as it often had before. She wondered where he'd learned to use it, and she knew that he must have had sex with other women before they were married. How else would he know all the things he did?

For Catherine, it was a relief that he was responding so keenly to her body; since they'd come to Fort Bridge, he seemed to be devoting all his concentration to his research and very little to her. She was afraid that, despite having only been married eight months, they were somehow drifting apart from each other in a subtle way, Jefferson being lured from her by his work toward the all-important PhD. In the evenings he was often too tired or busy with paperwork to give her the attention she needed, and recently they'd been making love very little. This bothered her, not because she felt an overwhelming need to make love, but because Jefferson's desire for her seemed to be diminishing. Was familiarity breeding contempt, or at least boredom, she wondered?

To calm the fears that were troubling her, Catherine leaned forward and kissed her husband hard on the mouth. He responded by thrusting his tongue in between her lips and swirling it around the moist cavern of her mouth. Still, a nagging worry gripped her. For some reason his responses seemed almost automatic, as though she had just become a habit and could no longer truly excite him. Perhaps if she could act even bolder, try something new, she would awaken his affection for her.

Catherine touched his lips to her own, placing small kisses on them and pulling gently at them with her teeth. Lulling him with her sweet caresses, she then darted her tongue deep between his lips, flicking the tip over his teeth and the roof of his mouth.

Jefferson teasingly pulled away and started to pull at the buttons on her shirt. "Why don't you take off some of these clothes? It's getting hot in here." She nodded silently, unable to reply as his hands glided around her thighs and cupped her firm ass clad in her little panties. Slipping his fingers higher, he grasped the frilly elastic waistband and pulled down, gliding his fingers over her bare, smoothly curving belly.

Squirming against him, Catherine nibbled his ear, her hands gripping tightly at his shirt. Then, with a teasing smile playing on her lips, she stepped back off the chair and stood a few feet in front of him, slowly unbuttoning her shirt and undoing her bra. Her beautiful breasts burst out of their confinement and stood firm, their pink, perfectly positioned nipples excited and hard.

Revelling in his excited gaze Catherine unzipped her miniskirt and stepped out of it. She could feel his impatience as she coyly hooked her fingers into the waistband of her half-rolled-down panties and completed the job, peeling them slowly down over her ripely rounded hips and thighs, letting them fall to her ankles and stepping out of them at last. Realising the power of her nubile young body, she slowly slid her palms down over the curves of her hips, smiling invitingly at her husband. Then, wordlessly, she lay down on the thickly carpeted floor, her sultry eyes inviting him to join her.

Jefferson slowly surveyed her near-perfect

form, her shining red hair tumbling down over one of her breasts, her soft, glistening skin lying white against the dark carpet. Her face was red from the passion of their argument, and her day-old make-up had worn and rubbed slightly, lending her eyes a smoky, sultry look. He could wait no longer and jumped up, wasting no time in ripping off his clothes, his engorged cock springing out from its confines and throbbing in anticipation.

Catherine could feel her almost uncontrollable excitement growing and wiggled her naked buttocks down against the carpet, revelling in the powerful effect her licentious actions were having on her husband.

Suddenly Jefferson was on top of her, his weight pushing her buttocks and thighs even deeper into the soft carpet. Catherine felt the tufts of carpet scraping the sensitive undersides of her thighs and bringing ripple after ripple of lewd delight through her loins.

"Ummmh, you certainly work fast, don't you?" she whispered heatedly in his ear.

"I've been ready for this the last twenty minutes. You sure as hell know how to turn on a guy," he said, grinning down at her, his hands running feverishly over her ripely straining breasts, then down her sides and over her thighs. They moved up again until his fingers were pinching at her nipples, causing them to swell up into hard little darts of sensitivity until she almost wanted to groan from the exquisite pain.

Lifting his head for a moment, Jefferson ran his eyes over her lushly curvaceous body, feasting on what he saw. She still excited him like no other woman in the world. In truth, he had worried that he would grow easily bored of the physical side of their relationship after a few months, but she'd managed to hold his interest. Everything about her was designed for sex, even that unconsciously sultry face of hers with its full, slightly pouting lips and those wide, deep, green eyes. He could still recall their first meeting and the electrical charges running through his body when he laid eyes on her. Like now, the way her mouth was slightly open! God, there was nothing more he would have liked to do than put his rock-hard cock between her wetly parted lips and have her suck him off, but she had been stubborn about some forms of sex from the beginning and was stubborn even now that they were man and wife.

He'd gone so far as to suggest oral sex once or twice, but she had simply shuddered with revulsion and loathing. In spite of this disappointment, he had to admit she was coming along, learning more and more about lovemaking each day under his tutelage. His gaze drifted down to her softly curling pussy-hair, all coppery-coloured and glinting in the light. He could see the pink succulent flesh of her pussy moistly gleaming from the excited secretions of passion which had already formed on her cunt-lips. Maybe there would be a breakthrough today; she seemed bolder and more open today. Maybe he could convince her to try something new and different. Who knows? Maybe he might turn her into a completely uninhibited mistress after all.

Without warning, Jefferson slid down between her open legs and suddenly, on an impulse, clamped his hungrily watering mouth over her squirming vaginal mound, his tongue licking forward in between the wet inviting crease of her hotly clasping pussy, his upper lip brushing against the erected column of her clit. She moaned and suddenly drew her legs together.

"No, Jefferson, no! Please, don't do that." She squirmed and tried to push him away, her tone becoming desperate, as though she realised she had teased him too much. She hadn't meant for him to go this far... oh, God! It just wasn't right. "Jefferson, don't kiss me there, please."

There was no use trying to resist her. He knew she would just panic and push him away, and that would ruin everything. He had to take things easy, he realised, and furthermore, even though the sensually enticing redhead had been giving him a strong come-on, this obviously wasn't the right time to push matters. Damn, how could she have such a ripely inviting body and be so afraid of sex at the same time? It was enough to drive him crazy. If only she could understand the wonderful variety of sexual pleasures that were available, things would be so much better. If only once she would let herself go and allow him to stick his tongue up inside the sweet moisture of her tight little cunt! He wanted to see her lose that haughty pride of hers and just let go, writhing and squealing in ecstasy as he tongue-fucked her with all his might. He wanted to see her parting those full pouting lips and suck his cock deep into her throat, gurgling with pleasure as he began a slow rhythmic fucking motion in and out of her mouth. But no, it was all just a dream. She would never do any of it.

As his imagination ran away into wild erotic fantasies, he could feel her naked belly grinding in impatience up against his pelvis, searching for his thickly bulging penis, which was rubbing against her navel.

"Oh, sweetheart, I want you... I want you so much," she moaned passionately, her eyes clenched tightly shut. "Give it to me now!"

"Yes, I want you too," he whispered, but it was almost mechanical. He wished his daydreams could come true, that she would indulge in the wild, wanton things he wanted her to do, but he knew it would end up the same as it always had been... the same unoriginal, conventional sex.

"What's the matter? Is there something wrong?" she asked softly, a touch of hurt in her eyes.

"No, nothing," he said flatly. "Nothing's wrong." ...

Catherine began to respond more fervently now, her hips bobbing up against his throbbing maleness. "Please, do it, stick it inside me," she murmured throatily. "I need it... please."

Maybe she did need it after all, he thought. She certainly sounded convincing, and he could feel a surge of renewed excitement speeding through his loins. Her tremulous plea sent his long, hard cock throbbing, aching to penetrate the soft, warm depths of her tightly clasping pussy.

Catherine writhed up against him as she grasped his rock-hard buttocks and pulled him tighter against her naked body. Blushing, she reached down between them and grasped his rigidly pulsating penis. Slowly, tantalisingly, she clasped her hand around it, rubbing it up and down, feeling the virile organ respond to her tender ministrations, growing thicker and more bulbous with each rhythmic pull she made. Carefully she guided it to the gaping lips of her wetly quivering cunt.

"Now, now!" she begged.

In answer to her plea he lunged his hips suddenly forward, thrusting the lust-swollen shaft into her heated, wet vagina.

"Oooooh, oh, oh!" she gasped, her body jerking as she thrust her pelvis upward in unrestrained eagerness to meet his lust-thickening shaft of flesh. His pulsating cock slammed up into the very depths of her vagina, and when its mushroomed head scraped across her cervix, she trembled from head to toe as wildly ecstatic sensations surged all through her body. She could feel her hotly quivering pussy growing wetter each second as he rammed up into her, his sperm-bloated testicles slamming against her churning buttocks. Catherine squealed in lewd delight as he withdrew, and then with a twitch of his hips thrust in again, grinding against her in a savage rhythm as his teeth nipped at the flesh of her neck. She strained to meet each pounding thrust, mewling and groaning in rapturous desire as his buttocks flexed and hollowed to drive his thick, rigid hardness up into her liquid heat. Her pussy lips clasped frantically around his penis and her deeper vaginal muscles rippled in an effort to pull it further up into her belly.

"Uggggggh, ummmh," she cried. "Yes,

yes, it's beautiful." Her head twisted on the carpet from side to side, her long red tresses sweeping against the thick, shaggy carpet in rhythm to the buffeting of her body. Her mind was lost in dizzying spirals of ecstasy, and her legs opened and closed around his hips as she bucked and churned beneath him, arching her body upward so that she could suck his rigidly thrusting cock deeper inside her vagina. She let herself go in total abandon and for the moment became a wild animal desiring nothing but to be fucked by his long, hard penis. God, how badly she wanted its pulsating thickness deeper and deeper inside her.

Jefferson looked down at his wife as she writhed and churned on the floor, moaning and wailing, her head flailing from side to side in wanton abandon. Her lips were moistly parted and she was chanting savage grunts as he fucked in and out of her clasping young pussy. His tempo increased as she dug her heels into the small of his back to spur him on. Sensing that she was rapidly approaching climax, he dug his fingernails into the soft flesh of her buttocks and squeezed with all his might, bringing savage wails of pleasure-pain from her lips. He thrust deeper and harder, his muscles tensing, his huge organ bulging and flexing inside her tight little cunt.

"Harder, harder, baby!" he urged,

slamming into her. "Shake it, move your ass, you bitch!"

The cruel shock of his vulgar words nearly halted her orgasm, but she had gone too far already – the only thing that mattered was her husband's deliciously throbbing penis planted deep in between her legs. She felt like an animal now, a savage animal who cared about nothing except being fucked.

"Oooh, unnnghhh!" she wailed, as loud sucking noises emanated from her hotly skewered pussy with each powerful thrust of his thick, rigid cock up into her vaginal passage. She could hear his sperm-laden balls smacking against her nakedly quivering buttocks, and they felt as though they were weighted with lead. Finally, it was too much to bear, and she could feel herself collapsing before his masculine onslaught, her mind reeling and spinning from the overpowering sensations that were invading her body.

Her body began to shudder and shake, she groaned and trembled, her legs jackknifing up and out, her feet pointed up toward the ceiling.

"Y-yesss, oh God, yesss, fuck me!" she sputtered, the vulgar word escaping involuntarily from her lips. "Oh... oh God! I'm coming!"

Feeling his wife straining with all her might toward orgasm, Jefferson jerked and thrust his body against hers, his burgeoning cock burrowing deeper and deeper into the tightly clasping warmth of her vagina, flexing and pulsing in mad spasms of uncontrollable lust. He couldn't hold it any longer. His body shuddered, and suddenly the boiling hot sperm stored in his cum-filled testicles rocketed out from the swollen tip of his penis deep into the wet heat of her tight young cunt. His fingernails raked her nakedly twisting ass-cheeks, his belly slapped with a leathery thud against hers, and his face contorted into a mask of savage desire. With a groan his cum rocketed into her belly like sharp bursts of machine gun bullets, making her writhe and twitch beneath him.

And almost as suddenly as it had begun it was over. The two of them lay quietly, silently, on the carpet, their sweat-streaked bodies trembling, their chests heaving as they gasped for breath. Finally Catherine opened her eyes and looked up at him with a broad, contented smile on her face.

"That was nice, wasn't it?" she purred. "Oh, Jefferson, I love you so much."

Yeah, it was nice all right, he thought. He could not, again, help feeling disappointed. It would have been so much better if she had just let me try something new, if she would just let herself relax and accept what I was willing to do for her. His returning annoyance grew quickly to anger as he thought about his wife's selfishness and narrow-minded prudery.

"I... I'd better get up now," he heard her say. "I should start making dinner."

"Screw dinner," he growled with a savagery that surprised even himself. "We just started our fucking contest!"

For once he wished she would think about him instead of dinner, a job, or whatever else was bugging her. He wished she would just relax and enjoy sex to the fullest. All right, he admitted to himself, he wanted a good wife, but at the same time, he wanted a wife who could really get into the pleasures of sex and not just pretend that she was interested. It's just my luck, he thought, to end up with an incredibly sexy woman who doesn't seem to give a damn about sex, who can take it or leave it as she pleases.

His limp cock was still lodged in her moist, warm vagina and he could feel the tender little lips of her pussy rubbing against its base as he rearranged himself on top of her. Hell, with a little bit of excitement, he could give it to her again, and even now he could feel it beginning to twitch as it began to rejuvenate itself. His frustration at her apparent lack of interest even seemed to help it along. Hell, he was going to give it to her once again just to prove who was boss, and it didn't matter whether she liked it or not.

Suddenly he raised up his hips and slammed into her, feeling his cock responding almost immediately. It grew slightly harder, awakening to the spasmodic twitching of her cunt-lips. Catherine gasped as her breath escaped from her chest with the unexpected thrust. She could feel the heated moisture of their orgasms already leaking out of her vagina, around her husband's cock and down the sides of her thighs. How could he want to make love to her again, she wondered? She must have worked him up to a fever pitch.

Her thoughts were disrupted, however, as his penis began to swell up to its former size and slip easily in and out of the rubbery wetness of her vagina. She knew he was using her like a cheap slut, but in truth she was consumed with a burning hunger for his penis. God, how she wanted him! Jefferson, for his part, felt himself growing more annoyed by the second as he saw his wife responding to the thrusts of his resurrected organ. He had meant to punish her, but it wasn't working the way he'd expected. She was actually enjoying it. She actually wanted him to fuck her again! Christ, he wished he could stick his cock in her mouth, forcing it down her throat. That would really show her something, but he knew it would be futile even now, when she was aroused to an abnormal degree. He had to make do with what she was offering him and so, jerking his hips, he thrust into her again, venting his anger as he used her body as a mere receptacle for his loins.

He felt his wife straining toward orgasm a second time. Pushing harder, he fucked into her in complete abandon beneath him and then, suddenly, he stopped. This was no different than it had ever been before.

"W-what's the matter?" she stammered, a confused look in her eyes.

"I'm getting tired of the same old thing," he breathed angrily. "I want something new. Turn over."

"W-what do you mean? What do you want?"

"Just turn over," he commanded her. "Do what I say."

She could see he was angry now, and without protest obeyed his order, rolling nakedly over onto her belly as his hands clamped around and raised her buttocks high in the air. She was on her knees, helplessly held in place, afraid of what was going to happen next.

"Jefferson, what are you going to do?"

"I'm going to fuck you real good," he said firmly. "I'm going to show you how good it can be."

Staring down at her sensually rounded buttocks, he felt a wave of lust sweep over him, revelling in the idea of his young bride kneeling in submission before him. He knew she was going to think it would be dirty, but so much the better. He was getting tired of her prudish outlook on sex. Catherine cringed as her husband stretched wide the twin mounds of her buttocks until she could feel a cool rush of air flowing into the crevice. What was he doing? Was he actually going to take her from the rear, like an animal? A bitch on heat?

"Relax, goddammit," he hissed at her. "I'm going to slide it in nice and easy, baby, and you're going to love it."

He moved forward, guiding his cock into the moistened entrance of her hair-lined cunt with thumb and forefinger, until his belly was up against her buttocks.

"Oh, Jefferson!" she cried as she felt the blunt-tipped staff of flesh suddenly ram up inside her, sliding powerfully forward until it scraped against her cervix. He'd never gone this far inside her before... it was too much! She couldn't stand it.

But the young husband's strength was overpowering, and his thumbs prised her naked ass-cheeks wider and wider apart as he jerked his cock inside her hotly throbbing cunt. Her struggles only seemed to excite him more as her vaginal muscles involuntarily clasped and unclasped around the throbbing organ which bulged and grew inside her like an organism with a life of its own.

Her humiliation was beyond belief. She was kneeling before him like a slave, cringing and submitting to his depraved desires. Her face was flushed, her lush red hair swept over her back and shoulders as her head bobbed from side to side. Her arms strained against the carpet as she tried to support herself from the thrusts he was making into her belly. It was vile, obscene, but there was no way to escape. Oh God! What had come over him? Why was her own husband doing this to her?

Behind her, Jefferson's eyes gleamed with wanton desire as he watched his wetly glistening penis disappear into the heated depths of her cringing little cunt. His excitement mounted, his body was alive and tense with savage feeling, his muscles quivering as he strained to give her the fucking of her life. The ragged pink edges of her vaginal lips clung to his thick shaft on the out-stroke and then it disappeared back inside the hair-lined little opening as he rammed hard into her, bringing cries of impassioned ecstasy from her throat. His balls were aching and crying out for relief, and his hips slammed tight against her wildly churning buttocks, jerking her forward as his hands gripped the soft flesh of her hips, holding her fast to his loins.

Bending forward over her, he reached

down and seized her heavily swaying breasts, cupping and squeezing their soft, warm resilience in his hands until he brought cries of protest from her throat. Goddamn, she was a sexy little bitch and he wanted to pump his sperm as far up into her belly as it could go. He pulled her back tight against him as he pistoned his pulsating hardness inside her tight cunt passage. He was almost there as he began bucking and thrusting like a stallion now, gritting his teeth together, his face grimacing as low moans of anguished pleasure burst from his throat.

Catherine was whining and mewling before him, but his mind had been taken over completely by his body, and he was a naked animal jerking and humping with an instinctive passion on the ripe white buttocks before him.

In spite of the humiliation, Catherine could feel him penetrating deeper and deeper into the innermost regions of her cunt, making her whole body twitch and throb with an uncontrollable passion. She moaned and babbled, shaking her head from side to side, grinding her hands into the carpet. Her buttocks bucked back against his groin, her stomach trembled and she let her legs slide wider and wider apart. It will be over soon, she kept telling herself, but still she could feel tremulous jolts of pleasure coursing all through every nerve ending, and the horrible thought came to her that she was actually enjoying being used as a slut.

He was fucking faster and faster, his huge male organ throbbing and jerking, and suddenly he threw his head back, uttering a deep, desperate groan as his penis flexed and began spitting long, hot jets of cum into the kneeling young wife's hotly clasping pussy. She jerked and twisted her ass-cheeks in teasingly rotating circles, trying to capture every last ounce of sperm that he was pumping into her. Her buttocks slammed against his stomach as he rocketed hot, quick shots of cum far up inside her.

"Whew!" he breathed finally. "That was wild. Jesus, that was wild."

Catherine collapsed on the carpet flat on her stomach, trying to gather her scattered thoughts. Her breasts and nipples ached from the intensity of her husband's manipulations, and her vagina throbbed from his battering-ram thrusts. Though not really angry, she was puzzled by her husband's insensitive, animalistic treatment of her, and especially by the fact that he seemed to have enjoyed what he had done. But how could she protest? She was his wife, and it was her duty to please him. Still, it was unfair of him to force her to do something that she felt was dirty, even immoral. Had he really been so bored with her that he had to insist on perverted things like what he had just done? She turned over onto her back, lying alongside him.

"Jefferson... why did you want me to do it that way?"

He smiled contentedly. "We just needed something different, that's all. Variety's the spice of life, isn't it?"

He glided his hand along the curve of her lips one last time, letting it linger for a moment, and then he got up and headed into the bathroom. So, he really was bored with her, she said to herself. She felt miserable now, being blatantly used as a sex object and then being told that all along she'd been inadequate for his needs. She moved over to the chair and curled up under Jefferson's shirt, her pussy leaking a delicate trail of moisture. Confused and tired, she shut her eyes. God, what would he make her do next?

Chapter 2

Catherine could barely conceal her nervousness as she stood in the hallway of the Ellsworth-Cima Research Centre and knocked timidly on the door marked 'Director'. Around her, trim-looking research workers in white coats and carrying clipboards were busily scurrying to and fro with purposeful expressions on their faces. It was nearly nine, time for her rendez-vous with Dr Stephen Marlingham, and she certainly hoped he wouldn't have forgotten about it. Why should he, though, Catherine wondered. After all, she had called him the previous day and he seemed quite enthusiastic about her coming to work for him.

As she looked at the efficient, crisp-looking people passing by, she felt somewhat out of place and yet anxious to be a part of their world. After all, she had been an honours student in biology and was perfectly capable of getting a Masters degree herself. Who knows, she thought, maybe this job might lead somewhere, even if it was just an administrative position.

"Well, hello there, Mrs Peterson," a deep voice boomed from behind her. "I see you're right on schedule."

Spinning around, she nearly crashed into the broad, imposing figure of Dr Stephen Marlingham, who greeted her with a rugged smile.

"Oh, I'm sorry. You startled me. I thought you would be inside your office."

"I was just heading there," he said jovially, swinging the door open and letting her enter. She went in halfway, waiting for him to follow, but for some reason he lingered right where he was, and in a second, Catherine could see why. He was gazing at a tall, shapely female researcher heading down the corridor in his direction. The girl was wearing dark-framed glasses and her dark hair was tied back in a bun. As she passed in front of the director, Stephen Marlingham reached out and grasped one of her buttocks, a playful grin on his face. Catherine was startled that the director of the Ellsworth-Cima Research Centre would do something like that, but she was even more startled when the girl turned around and chuckled playfully.

"Doctor, not this early in the morning."

"I always like a little dessert before I eat breakfast," he grinned, and then turned to usher Catherine inside.

"Wonderful girl," Marlingham said appreciatively as he strode over to his desk, oblivious to the shocked look on Catherine's face. "She's got a body like a call-girl and a brain like Einstein."

My God, Catherine thought, maybe I have made a mistake. Maybe Jefferson was right about Marlingham being an old lecher who would chase me around the desk all day. How could a responsible scientist be so intimate with one of his researchers? It just wasn't right.

"For goodness sake, dear lady. Sit down," Marlingham chided her as she stood nervously in front of his desk.

"Y-yes sir," she stammered, still confused, but immediately obeying his order.

"Don't call me sir and don't call me doctor," he insisted. "Call me Stephen and I'll call you Catherine. We're all on a first name basis here."

"Yes, Doctor... I mean, Stephen."

"Good, that's much better. Now tell me something. How long have you been married to that husband of yours?"

"Six months," she replied to the unexpected question.

"Umm... does he service you well?"

'Service me well'? What in the world did he mean by that, Catherine asked herself in shocked surprise. Is he asking me to tell him about the intimacies of my sex life? And yet she could see he wasn't just making some sort of crude joke. He fully expected an answer.

"I... I don't know what you mean."

"Come, come, you know exactly what I mean. It's just a clinical question. Do you know what we do at the Ellsworth-Cima Research Centre all day? We watch fish and crabs having intercourse with each other. It's a nice change to talk about people doing it once in a while."

Catherine's mouth gaped open as she tried to convince herself she was not living in a dream. It was too incredible to be true that a respected scientist whom she'd only met once would be asking her questions about her sex life. She could feel a hot blush rising to her cheeks as he stared at her without the slightest trace of embarrassment.

"Never mind," he said finally. "I can see you're the prudish type."

The young redhead stammered without saying anything and squirmed uncomfortably in her chair. Stephen Marlingham's eyes were burning into her like hot coals, raking lewdly over her body as though trying to penetrate her clothing. For a moment she felt like rising from her chair and suddenly running from the room, but a kind of weird fascination took hold of her. She felt herself falling into the grip of the director's presence, tiny pleasant sensations welling in her body just from the prurient way he was staring at her.

"Relax," Marlingham said at last. "I always make jokes. I just wanted to break the ice. Can't stand formality, damn it."

What kind of game was he playing, she wondered. His lecherous gaze of a moment ago had simply disappeared and now he was sporting a kind, fatherly look on his face. He seemed so calm and self-possessed it was difficult to believe he had asked her such a shocking question just a moment ago.

"I'm sorry," she apologised. "You just caught me off guard, that's all."

"Oh now, don't worry about it. We'll start

you working right away, and then you'll get into the swing of things. Your desk is right over there."

Catherine twisted around and peered over her shoulder at a small desk in one corner of the room. A computer was sitting on it, but otherwise it was clear.

"To begin with, you'll be doing mostly my correspondence and filing, and then as you familiarise yourself with how things run I'll give you more responsibilities. My last secretary left rather abruptly, so I suggest you clean out the desk first thing. After that, there are some letters to be typed... they're in my out basket. Okay, you have enough to do for a while. I should be back shortly."

Briskly, Marlingham rose from his desk, waved goodbye and headed out the door, leaving Catherine to breathe a sigh of relief. Thank God, he had a normal side to him after all. But still, he was certainly an eccentric. Undoubtedly he was just a harmless, middle-aged man who enjoyed engaging in flirtation with his female staff, something that could prove annoying, though it certainly wasn't dangerous, she reassured herself.

Still recovering from her shock, Catherine lingered for a moment in the chair by the desk. She tried to think of something pleasant to calm her nerves, but the only thing that came to her mind was the memory of the previous weekend, when she and Jefferson had made love so beautifully at first and then he had taken her from the rear with blind disregard for her feelings. After he'd done it, she began to think that perhaps it wasn't really wrong after all and the next time she would force herself actually to enjoy it.

That very same night, though, he'd done something that completely put her off. Shortly after dinner, when she was still bruised and aching from his manhandling, he had tried to make her suck and kiss his penis in spite of her protests. Even now the very thought of something so disgusting and degrading made her feel sick to the stomach. She hadn't done it, of course. She had fought and protested every inch of the way and finally blown up at him, which didn't do any good either, because he grew angry in turn and began calling her a frigid bitch. Now he was sulking, giving her the cold shoulder, but what did it matter? She wasn't going to act like a common slut for him or anyone else. There were certain principles she just wasn't going to sacrifice to satisfy her husband's male, animal needs. He would just have to learn how to control himself, and that was that.

It was time to stop brooding, she told herself, and get to work, and so she headed over to the typing desk, sliding into the swivel chair and pulling open the top drawer. Sorting through the contents, she found pads, pencils, paper clips, and other sundry equipment; the previous secretary really seemed to have left in a hurry, Catherine thought, as she found a make-up compact and a half-full pack of cigarettes. After cleaning and rearranging the drawer, she went on to the next one, finding it completely empty except for an unsealed manila envelope. There was no name on it, and it didn't appear to be anyone's private property, so out of curiosity she bent back the metal clasp and opened it.

A packet of full-colour photographic prints slid out and spilled over the desk, much to her surprise. She knew now they were none of her business, but she couldn't help looking at them, and when she did the sight nearly blew her mind. She gasped in horror as she stared at the top print, feeling her heart pounding in her throat. There in perfect focus and brilliant colour was a photograph of a man and a woman locked in a lewd, vile embrace. They were sprawled on a bed with the woman's head in between the man's legs and her lips locked around his big, swollen penis. The man, for his part, had likewise buried his head between her thighs and obviously had his mouth on her vagina.

"Oh God," she gasped as her eyes dwelled on the expression on the woman's face. She was actually enjoying what she was doing.

Her eyes glowed with rapture, her face was twisted in a lewd grimace of abandoned frenzy. It was sick, disgusting! It almost made her want to throw up, and quickly she gathered up the photos and slipped them back into the envelope. But what would she do with it? She couldn't throw it away, because after all it was someone else's private property, and she certainly wasn't going to mention the matter to Stephen Marlingham. No, the only thing to do was to leave the envelope with its filthy contents right where it was. She certainly hadn't put it there to begin with, and there was no way she could be held responsible.

She was just about to place the envelope back in the drawer when a kind of perverse curiosity overcame her. She had no idea what was behind it, but she found herself reopening the clasp once again, as though her hands were being manoeuvred by some sinister, invisible force. Her fingers trembling, she set the first photo aside and fixed her eyes on the second one in the series. The same girl was now crouching on the floor between the wide-splayed legs of the man, who was sitting on the edge of the bed. Her mouth was tightly wrapped around his thickly protruding cock, and her fingers were cupping his testicles. The expression on her face was taut and intense, and it looked as though she was in the process of actually swallowing the sperm-inflated organ.

Catherine closed her eyes tightly shut as her body trembled with strange sensations. She knew the photos were lewd and disgusting, but somehow they were making her loins and belly churn, sending charges of excitement to the farthest reaches of her fingertips. It was almost as though Jefferson and she were in bed together making love.

I can't look at these, she told herself, trying to avert her eyes. Her conscience screamed at her, telling her to throw the photos away, but her hands merely trembled, as though locked in some sort of weird paralysis. She glanced up at the door to see if anyone might be coming, but it was safe, and though she knew it was wrong, continued to flip hurriedly through the rest. The lewd, vile positions that she saw filled her with loathing and quivering excitement at the same time. The woman was contorted in strange positions, sometimes being violated by two and three men. God, it was sick. Who in the world would keep photos like this in his desk? Had the former secretary been some sort of pervert, or had Stephen Marlingham planted these photos there as a strange practical joke? If so, he certainly had an offbeat sense of humour, and he was a man she would always have to be on her guard against.

The last photo was the most shocking, and she dwelled on it longer than the others.

It showed the woman with her legs spread wide on the bed, her head tilted back and a rapturous expression on her face. Her fingers were lodged tightly inside her vagina as she attempted to satisfy herself without a man, and for some reason Catherine found this spectacle more perverted than the others.

It was a good thing there was no one in the office at that moment, because she could feel her excitement mounting by the second. Mesmerised by the lewd photographs, she found her hand involuntarily moving up toward her left breast. She began squeezing it in a gentle, sensual rhythm until her nipple swelled in response, and then, though she hardly knew what she was doing, her free hand slipped under her skirt and up in between her thighs so that her fingertips were brushing tantalisingly against her silken panty crotchband. Trembling with anticipation, she slipped the legband aside and made contact with her finger against her slightly moistened cunt-lips. My God, what am I doing? she suddenly said to herself as she realised what was happening. She had been so carried away that she was unconsciously mimicking the action of the woman in the last snapshot.

Abruptly she sat straight in her chair and came to again, having heard noises in the outside hallway. Fortunately, no one seemed to be heading toward the office, and she breathed a sigh of relief. Thank God she'd caught herself. There was no telling what she might have done. Shuddering at the depraved horror of what had almost happened, she gathered up the photographs once again, slipped them back in the envelope and, once the envelope was in the drawer, slammed it tightly shut. Perhaps Jefferson had been right after all. Perhaps she should have just contented herself with staying at home and being a good wife.

* * *

Catherine had finished the letters by the time the director returned. He was accompanied by a man who identified himself as an executive with a large philanthropic foundation, a foundation which had supplied a good deal of money to the Ellsworth-Cima Research Centre to finance its scientific projects. By now she had managed to still the unaccustomed sexual sensations that had welled inside her as she viewed the lewd photographs.

During the wait for his return she'd asked herself over and over again whether she should bring up anything concerning the photos, but after a long battle with her conscience she had come to the conclusion that it was better not to. Marlingham might just laugh at her and, even worse, word might somehow spread through the office grapevine to her husband.

In fact, she'd even resolved not to tell Jefferson about what she'd discovered. The way he was acting lately, he might even probe her on the subject and then suggest they try to duplicate some of the poses she'd seen. No, she wouldn't put it past him at all. This was one incident she was going to keep entirely to herself.

The man from the foundation and Marlingham had seated themselves around his desk and began their conversation in low tones, which led Catherine to think that maybe they wanted to speak privately.

"Excuse me, Dr Marlingham," she said politely, spinning around in her swivel chair. "Would you like me to come back in a couple of minutes?"

The director looked up at her, a wide grin crossing his face. "Why don't you go down to the canteen and bring a couple of cups of coffee back?" he said jovially, winking at her.

"Yes, sir," Catherine replied, embarrassed at being reduced to the status of a servant. Why did she have to get coffee just because she was a woman? Well, she couldn't protest about it now in the presence of a visitor on her first day on the job, but she was determined to mention it sometime to the arrogant scientist.

The canteen, which was down the corridor, was actually a cluster of vending machines, and five minutes later, Catherine returned with two plastic containers of coffee. Just as she was about to tap on the door with her foot, she could hear loud guffaws booming inside the office. The laughter was raucous, almost as if the two men had been exchanging dirty jokes, and motivated by curiosity, she lingered outside the door trying to overhear what they were saying. The more she knew about Stephen Marlingham, the better it would be, she told herself. He was certainly a strange individual who seemed to have multiple sides to his personality.

"So what happened then?" she heard Marlingham bellowing with delight. The voice broke into loud chuckles, then continued, "No, I can't believe it."

"Stephen, you know I wouldn't tell you a lie," the other man cackled. "Hell, I walked right in on them. He had that hot little bitch spread right out on the floor of his office, and by God was he giving it to her. He was fucking her like a stallion. Right during office hours with me standing there looking at the both of them."

"Well, it looks like you people have some fun up there, but I still say it can't compare to down here. Hell, I had two new researchers in here sucking me off just last week – right here in my office."

"Chrissake, Stephen, you don't slow down at all," the other man laughed loudly.

Catherine's eyes were wide with disgust and horror. So Marlingham really was a dirty old man after all, the proof being in what she'd just heard. And the other man – a representative of a philanthropic foundation – was no better. They were both vile, lewd people laughing and guffawing at incredibly sick things. What was the world coming to? Her mind was made up now, for no matter how important the idea of having a job was to her, she just couldn't stay here any longer. In fact, she didn't even want to face those two men at all now, or even later. She just couldn't walk in and pretend that she hadn't heard anything, pretend that she was just a dumb secretary who should be content with serving coffee and not keeping her ears open at all.

Just as she was about to turn away from the door, however, she could hear the director's voice again.

"Hell," he snorted, "people think scientific research institutes are dull, sterile places. If they could ever see what goes on here at Ellsworth-Cima, they'd sure as hell change their minds quick. Those young broads with their Masters degrees are the horniest females I've ever seen."

"Stephen, you make me envious," the other man said, and once again the voices in the room broke out into a chorus of laughter.

"Come to think of it, Bill, it's not only our budding young female scientists who turn me on. Hell, I just hired a young secretary today, and damn, you should see her body. She's built like a brick shithouse, but she's as uptight as they come. She'll come around, though, believe me. It'll take a little bit of work but she'll come around just like they all do."

Catherine recoiled from the door as she heard these last words and nearly spilled the coffee on the corridor floor. Could she really believe what she was hearing? Was Stephen Marlingham actually talking about her? What did he mean she would come around? So Jefferson was right after all. Marlingham was a notorious lecher, not just some kind of flirtatious middle-aged jokester. Jefferson had been right about trying to keep her from taking a job at the Centre, and now she owed him an apology. Hurrying down the hall, she jettisoned the coffee cups in a wastebasket and made straight for the laboratory where he was working.

Chapter 3

An hour or so earlier that day Jefferson had
gone to his customary lab, which was located
adjacent to the staff lounge downstairs. To his
surprise, he found that he had company.

"I'm Jennifer Wilson," the shapely,
dark-haired girl said, removing her glasses
and giving him a warm smile.

"Well, what a surprise. I've been getting
used to working by myself. I'm glad to have
some company. What are you working on?"

"The sea bass," she said, pointing at one
of the aquariums that was built into a wall of
the room. "Would you like some coffee?"

"Please, thanks."

As the white-coated researcher ambled
over to one of the lab tables to boil some
water over a bunsen burner, Jefferson's eyes
riveted on her ripe, sensual body. Jesus, she
really swung those hips when she walked.
And to look at her from a distance you would
think she was just some sort of cold-hearted,
intellectual bitch, the way she wore her hair
tied back and those dark-framed glasses
perched on her nose. She certainly seemed
friendly enough, Jefferson thought, but how
friendly she was he didn't find out until she

came back with the coffee and sat down facing him on the lone table that spanned the side of the room where the aquariums were located.

"It must be like solitary confinement, working in here alone all the time," she said sympathetically, handing over his cup.

He noticed that she had taken her glasses off and crossed her legs with a swishing of nylon, the skirts of her lab coat falling away so that he got a good glimpse of smoothly attractive thighs. Was he crazy or did he sense a kind of impish glint in her eye?

"Don't you ever get ideas from watching those fish mate all the time?" she said unexpectedly.

"You mean ideas for my thesis?"

Jennifer tilted back her head and laughed.

"That wasn't exactly what I meant, but I suppose watching fish in an aquarium all day isn't the most stimulating thing in the world."

What did she mean? he wondered. Was it possible that she was flirting with him, had come here on purpose to flirt with him? He watched as she casually unbuttoned the top buttons of her coat, revealing a magnificent torso in a thin-knit halter top whose neckline drooped low enough to reveal a hint of her tantalising cleavage. Her breasts were full, high-set and bra-less, her tiny sharp-pointed nipples nearly bursting through the material.

"These lab coats make me feel silly," she said. "We don't really need them here, and they make you look so sterile."

Having made this announcement she slipped out of the white garment, stretching one leg out to support herself on the floor as she twisted her body. Jefferson's mouth fell agape as her short little skirt rode up above the level of her stocking garters, revealing a triangular expanse of silken panty material nestled between her thighs. God almighty, she had to know he was sitting there looking up between her legs, and yet she didn't seem in the least self-conscious about it. She even seemed to be taking an extra long time to get out of her lab coat. Whether this was part of the mating ritual of the scientific researcher, he wasn't sure, but he knew that his biological systems were operating smoothly, because he could feel his cock burgeoning in his pants. Jesus, she was a tempting piece, and she certainly knew how to put on the tease. What a pleasant surprise to see her here!

"I haven't seen you down here before, although I've certainly seen you around," he said, trying to find out what her real motivations were. She sipped her coffee, coyly swinging her legs over the edge of the table as though she were sitting on a riverbank.

"That's because I've never been here before. I decided to pay you a visit," she said with no trace of embarrassment, which completely blew Jefferson's mind. He could feel a blush rising to his face and searched vainly for the right words to say. He had never expected to be seduced in the world-renowned Ellsworth-Cima Research Centre, especially by a fellow scientist who just happened to be one of the most attractive females he'd ever seen. She was looking straight at him with soft eyes, her lips slightly parted as though eager to be kissed, and it was driving him absolutely crazy.

Unfortunately, at that moment, his thoughts went back to his wife and the difficult time they'd had over the weekend, when he had vainly tried forcing her to perform oral sex on him. There was nothing dirty about sucking your husband's cock, he'd insisted, but of course she'd put on her virginal act and fought him all the way. Damn, he was getting sick of her childish, puritanical views on sex and, what was worse, he was despairing of ever bringing her around no matter how hard he tried.

Well, screw her, he thought. This time he was just going to wait it out, give her one last chance. No more sweet talk, no more cajoling... he was just going to wait till she came to him. It was going to be one hell of a temptation, though, trying to keep his hands off this dark-haired beauty who had appeared from nowhere and pretty much said that she wanted to go to bed with him.

He loved Catherine, of course, in spite of her prudishness, but he was human after all, and the temptation in front of him now was a powerful one. Control yourself, Jefferson, he said inwardly. It'll just be trouble if you get involved with this chick. The Research Centre is a small place in a small town, and somebody's going to find out about it sooner or later.

Just as he had tried to strengthen his resolve with these thoughts, he saw Jennifer Wilson rising from the table and stretching her arms around the back of her head to undo the bun in her hair. There was a sultry, seductive look on her face, but she did it in complete silence, all the while her twinkling, dark eyes flashing at him. In a moment her tresses spilled free and cascaded over her shoulders as she ran her hands lightly through them.

"I look better this way, don't you think?" she said, slowly approaching the chair where he was sitting.

"I'm sure you look great any way," he said and smiled, loosening up for the first time.

"Do you really mean that? I hope so, because we can have a wonderful time together."

Before he knew what was happening the voluptuous researcher had grasped his hand and was leading him over to one of the lab tables. She seated herself on the edge, spreading her legs slightly apart and drawing him in between them.

"Well, if the fish can do it, why can't we?" she said huskily, making his cock leap and throb inside his pants.

"You mean, you want to – "

"Quiet, darling, just kiss me."

Jefferson hardly knew what to think, for by now his senses and all thoughts of his wife had deserted him. Bending forward, he grasped her hips and suddenly crushed his mouth down on hers, thrusting his tongue into the warm, moist cavern and being greeted by a passionate suction on her part. His restlessly stirring cock bulged and jerked, straining, like a wild animal with a life of its own, to burst loose from its confines. And, as tiny purring murmurs broke from her throat, her legs slithered around his hips, her feet locking together against the small of his back.

Never in his wildest dreams had he expected anything like this to happen. It was too incredible to be true. For days he had been thinking of Jennifer Wilson from a distance as a cold, crisp female scientist, but now he knew that she was a sex-charged animal who was turning him on the way he'd never been turned on before, not even by his own wife.

Suddenly she twisted her mouth away from his, and with her legs still locked around him leaned back at an angle, supporting herself with her arms behind her. Her luscious, stiff-nippled breasts heaved with each breath she took, and her long, dark hair dangled seductively over her shoulders.

"You didn't expect anything like this, did you?" she purred, a sultry smile flitting across her face.

"Hell, no," he said, barely able to contain his excitement.

"They never do. Well, don't worry. There's more in store for us. I feel awfully hot; why don't you lift my top up?"

His hands trembling, the young scientist obeyed, slipping his fingers into the waistband of her skirt and gliding the halter top upward over the tautly rounded flesh of her belly slowly, inch by tortured inch. The lower curve of her breasts emerged, white and voluptuously uplifted, and suddenly he knew if he went any further it would be all over; there would be no turning back.

"I... I can't," he stammered weakly. "I'm married. Besides, what would happen if somebody caught us in here? Christ, we'd lose our jobs."

She did not reply but merely gazed at

him, her lips slightly parted and glistening, as though silently challenging him to take her. You're not going to cop out now, she seemed to be saying, teasing him to go one step farther. How could he stop now, how could he possibly, even though he knew that his marriage and his PhD might be at stake if someone caught them in the act. The battle of his instincts against his conscience made him shake and tremble all over now, but finally his basest desires got the upper hand, and he rolled the halter top up so that it was bunched around her shoulders.

His eyes widened in stunned appreciation as his gaze fixed on her naked breasts. They gleamed like warm alabaster and thrust out proud, high on her chest, and her nipples were stiff with arousal. She drew him deeper in between her stocking-clad thighs. Her skirt had ridden up over her hips, revealing her frilly, white, lace panties and the bulging mound of her vagina contained within. Slowly she let her hand glide back along the edges of the lab table on either side until she was flat on her back, urging him on with her subtle gestures.

"Touch my breasts, touch them," she purred. Locked in her legs, his confined cock throbbing against her panty-cloaked loins, he bent forward from the hips and began gently running his fingers over her

nipples. Her eyes fluttered closed and she mewled with pleasure, slowly rolling her head from side to side and squirming her hips so that her vagina pressed even harder against the swollen maleness hidden in his trousers.

Jesus, he wanted to fuck her right here and now, but he hadn't completely lost his mind yet. His wife and his career still meant something to him, even though his willpower was slowly fading away second by frustrating second.

"We... we can't do it here. It's too dangerous."

In response she began slowly moving her shapely legs up and down along his sides, her thigh muscles flexing and unflexing in a slow, sensual rhythm.

"We can come back here after work," she said. "It will be perfectly safe. No one will see us, of course, unless you don't want to." His mind was boiling with mad confusion, his conscience and his lust tearing at him from both directions, his hands kneading and squeezing her soft, pliable breasts, kneading them like dough and feeling the tight little buttons of her nipples pressing into his palms. Suddenly, like an animal sensing danger, he jumped back and spun around toward the door of the lab.

"What was that noise?" he said nervously.

He was positive that he had heard something, positive that he'd heard the door click shut.

Chapter 4

Catherine raced through the deserted staff lounge adjoining the lab, through the corridors and back toward her office on the ground floor, all the while fighting back the tears that were threatening to burst from her eyes. She dashed inside and hurriedly seated herself at her desk, which faced away from the director's.

"My God, what's wrong with you?" Marlingham called out to her in his booming voice. "What happened? You said you were bringing us some coffee and then you disappeared."

Even though Marlingham's voice was powerful, she could barely hear the words he was directing at her. Nothing was real now but the shattering scene she had witnessed between her husband and the woman in the lab. The image of the salacious spectacle bored through her mind like a hot firebrand, making her feel weak and dizzy. It couldn't be, it just couldn't. That awful woman with her legs wrapped around Jefferson's back, her breasts naked, mewling and grunting, as her husband massaged them with a vile, lecherous look on his face. She must be hallucinating! Jefferson could never do a thing like that. It must have been someone else, though her eyes had told her differently.

How long had it been going on? How many days had it taken for them to build up the intimacy of lovers that she had witnessed in the lab? And then a thought struck her. It must have been because of this other woman, this free-and-easy libertine, that Jefferson had insisted on her doing lewd things to him over the weekend. She had perverted him and aroused savage, carnal desires in his body. There was something wrong with this place, something wrong with everyone in it. For now, mixed up with the scene in the laboratory, was what she had overheard earlier – the foul, leering conversation between Marlingham and the man from the foundation, the horrible, dirty things they had said. Oh God, what had she gotten herself into? What was going to happen to her marriage?

"Catherine, for God's sake, what's wrong with you?" the director demanded from behind.

She started at the concerned tone of the older man's voice, which brought her suddenly back to reality. She remembered now that she had come back to announce that she was quitting immediately, but now everything was confused. If she left Jefferson, she would need a job to support herself. She couldn't quit. But no, that wasn't the real reason that she had suddenly lost her resolve. The real reason was that out of some morbid curiosity she desperately needed to find out who Jefferson was carrying on with and why. She had to discover how it had all happened.

"Catherine?"

The director's hand was on her shoulder; he was standing very close, and slowly she turned around to face him, trying to keep herself from flying to pieces. She couldn't tell him what was wrong. No, at all costs she had to keep the matter to herself. Forcing her voice to be calm, she replied with only a slight tremor, "It's… it's nothing. I just felt a little sick and didn't want to bother you. I feel much better now."

"Well, that's good. You had me worried for a minute. By the way, your husband called a minute ago and asked if I'd give you a message. He said he'd be working late tonight and to go ahead and eat without him."

She knew exactly what the message meant, of course, and even before Marlingham had finished the sentence she was sobbing uncontrollably. Bitter tears rolled down her cheeks, and she didn't resist as the brawny director eased her up from her chair and enfolded her in his arms.

"Now, now, Catherine. Tell me all about it. It will make you feel better."

As she started to unburden herself she couldn't see the smile of smug satisfaction that crossed the director's face. She was convinced that his sympathy was genuine and was sorry she had thought such awful things about him earlier.

"Don't worry about it, dear," he said. "I'll help you find out exactly what's happening."

Chapter 5

Jennifer Wilson re-entered the lab at five-thirty when the building had cleared, catching Jefferson as he glanced down at his watch.

"I'm here," she said breezily, striding over to him.

"Isn't there some way we could lock the door?" he said nervously.

"My, my, you are a scaredy-cat, aren't you? Don't worry, I took a quick look around, and almost everyone's gone. Anyone who's left won't come down here, that's for sure."

"What about the janitors?"

Jennifer chuckled.

"You should know by now: they work early in the mornings. Now just relax and let's have a drink."

Efficiently, the female researcher reached into the pockets of her lab coat and withdrew a flask of whisky and two paper coffee cups. A moment later they were toasting each other.

"I can see you really have no idea what goes on at the Centre, do you?" she said.

"What do you mean?"

"I'll explain sometime later. We have other things to do now."

After taking a sip of her drink Jennifer set it down on the lab table and slipped out of her white coat, much more quickly than she had done that morning. Jefferson's eyes fixed on her as tremors of nervous fear and excitement shot through his body. He felt like a young kid embarking on a dangerous adventure, and yet at the same time he knew damn well he wasn't going to refuse this incredible woman.

Hell, she'd done such a job of teasing him this morning, he'd been hard all day long and could hardly concentrate on his work. His cock right now felt like a telephone pole, and his balls were hanging as though they'd been stuffed with lead.

"W-where are we going to do it?" he said, trying to keep a grip on himself.

"On the lab table, of course," she said,

smiling mysteriously. "I have a thing about lab tables."

Jesus, she was a crazy one, but as far as he was concerned he'd do it anywhere with her, even swinging from a trapeze. He wondered what she meant about his not knowing what really went on at the Centre, but at the moment he was too excited to pursue the matter. He just wanted to sink his prick into that warmly waiting cunt of hers and damn the consequences.

Her hair was down to her shoulders now, and as she leaned against the edge of one of the tables, she undid her wide leather belt and let it drop to the floor with a clang.

"Why don't you help me?" she whispered. "I love to have men undress me."

As she said it, his rapidly awakening cock lurched inside his pants, and there was no longer any pretence of trying to keep it under control. It was making his pants bulge like a tent. In a flash, his fingers were undoing the zipper of her miniskirt and sliding it down over her ripely flaring hips. Ripples of excitement sped through his belly as the tiny garment dropped to her feet and she stepped out of it. Her slip came next, his thumbs hooking into the waistband and giving it a quick downward jerk.

Jennifer crossed her arms and lifted off her halter top and, at the same time,

Jefferson wrestled frantically to unsnap her garters and roll her nylons down over the smooth, cool skin of her legs. She was almost completely naked now, clad only in her brief bikini panties, the dark triangle of her pussy glimmering through the diaphanous material as she leaned back, shaking out her long, lustrous hair.

He couldn't stand it any more. He wanted to fuck her more than he'd ever wanted to fuck anyone in his life and, possessed by the driving animal need that was sparking his loins, he quickly stripped his clothes off and crushed his body against hers.

"Not so fast, we have plenty of time," she said soothingly. "First I want you to suck my pussy. You'll like that, won't you?"

Suck it? Jesus Christ, he'd ram his tongue all the way up inside her belly.

"This will be much more fun than watching sea bass," she murmured as she hopped up on the table, letting her long, lithe legs dangle over the edge and slowly spreading them apart as Jefferson instinctively sank to his knees. He gripped her knees tightly and then slid his hands over her smooth thighs until his fingertips were at the elastic of her panty waistband. Control yourself, he chided himself inwardly. You've got to go slow. If you do it too fast, you're gonna blow everything. All five fingers of each hand slid beneath the silk and began rolling it down over her hips. His hand grasped her nakedly churning buttocks, raised them up slightly, then glided the panties down over her legs. She sighed as he pulled them free of her ankles and then reclined so that she was lying flat on her back against the cold marble table.

"Suck me," she mewled. "Stick your tongue in my pussy."

He was mesmerised, hypnotised by her command. It was all so unreal that he should be urged by a beautiful, wanton woman to suck her pussy in the middle of a scientific laboratory. God, he'd never expected that a research job could be anything like this, and it was one hell of a pleasant surprise. What would Catherine do if she ever found out what was happening now? She'd go crazy, she'd go absolutely out of her mind.

His cock was aching and throbbing, the veins stretched, the mushroom-like head was bloated and swollen with blood, but he wasn't going to stick it in her, not yet, not until he had tongue-fucked her so that she was going insane on the table. Gripping her inner thighs tightly, he moved deeper in between her legs, suddenly stabbing his tongue between the wetly glistening folds of her cunt-lips. She jerked, a groan of delight tumbling from her throat, and her thighs spasmed tight around his temples.

"Oh God, yes, eat me, eat my pussy," she pleaded, her whole body trembling with eagerness.

* * *

Stephen Marlingham grinned slightly as he grasped the knob of the door in the staff lounge and turned it cautiously. He put his finger to his lips to caution the young redhead accompanying him, then motioned her over to where he was standing. The door was almost halfway open now, and they were both peering into the semi-darkness of the adjoining lab.

By now Catherine was perfectly under control, her green eyes sparkling with repressed anger as she scanned the lab, desperately hoping to find nothing that would shock her, though she knew something was definitely amiss.

"Remember now," the director whispered, "if you see anything, don't get hysterical, and don't try to stop them. You'll be sorry if you make a fool out of yourself and just barge in there. Besides, it wouldn't do to have a scene at the Centre. The word might get around somehow."

"Yes, yes, all right," she snapped impatiently in a hoarse whisper, gripping the edge of the door tightly with her fingers.

It was generous of him to help her like this, and she had to appreciate it, no matter how painful the situation turned out to be. He'd been so good to her, calming her down as she periodically burst into tears during the afternoon. But still, it was difficult to control her rising anger, and she couldn't help having directed it at him a second ago.

"Over there," Marlingham said suddenly, pointing in the direction of one of the tables, and immediately Catherine saw them. The salacious sight hit her with all the power of a fist in a stomach. Her eyes widened in horror as she sighted her naked husband down on his knees in between the widespread legs of the loudly groaning woman above him. His hands were gripping her thighs and his head was lewdly bobbing in and out from her loins. He was sucking and licking her vagina, obviously going at it with fervent passion as she twisted and writhed in ecstasy above him.

"Aaaggghh, ooh," the woman cried, uncontrollably squirming on the table-top, her legs locked tightly around his neck.

Catherine froze, her knuckles going white around the edge of the door. She was sure the kneeling man was her husband; there was no doubt about it, and she couldn't fool herself any longer. He was going all the way with this unknown woman, this whore, and she was going to witness every minute of it.

In the other room, Jefferson rose from his knees and slid Jennifer back along the table. Almost at once, he hopped up and mounted himself between her legs. Her hand reached down and gripped his heavily throbbing penis between her fingers, guiding it up toward her gaping pussy lips. A shudder of ecstasy went through his body as he felt the swollen tip of his cock pressing into the heated folds of her cunt, and then he took over for himself. Slowly flicking his hips forward, he inserted his rigidly pulsating member inch by inch into her tight young pussy.

"Ooh," she groaned as his lust-thickened organ throbbed and jerked deeper up inside her belly. She could feel it expanding even more as her cunt-lips clasped tightly and rippled around it.

Jefferson hovered over her on all fours, deliberately teasing her, wanting her to squirm and beg for it. He realised that he was completely in control now, all the power was with his body. He withdrew his pulsating hardness half an inch and thrust deep again, bringing a low moan from between her tightly clenched teeth as she spurred her heels into his spine.

Unable to believe the lewd scene she was witnessing, tears brimmed to Catherine's eyes. She gazed at the dark-haired woman obscenely rotating her pelvis and jerking her hips up toward Jefferson's pistoning penis. For the first time in her life she was seeing her husband have sex with another woman, and any way she looked at it, there was no denying that both of them were enjoying it to the fullest.

"Have you seen enough?" Marlingham said.

"No," she spat bitterly, "I want to see it all. I want to see everything."

"I don't think that's advisable."

Blinded by her tears, Catherine failed to notice the peculiar expression on the director's face. She could only think of herself and how she'd been hurt at the moment.

"I don't care. I want to see it all. I've never been so humiliated in my life." A slow, steaming anger was seething inside her, forcing back the tears that had formed from the shock of what she'd just seen. For just a second, Jefferson's warning about the director being a notorious skirt-chaser flashed through her mind, but why should she believe it now, when Jefferson himself was doing much more than chasing skirts, when he was cheating on her in the most blatant and obscene fashion imaginable!

Frozen in anger she watched as her husband bucked over the girl's churning body. How could he do this? How could he possibly do such lewd things with another woman?

He had not known the woman for more than a week or so, and yet they were engaging in intimacy which she and her husband had not practised even in all the months of their marriage.

Catherine's eyes bulged in hypnotic disbelief as her husband's lurching cock rammed in and out of the stranger's vagina, making loud, wet noises with each thrust. Desperately she wanted to scream and tear them apart, but in her state of shock she could only remain frozen at the half-open door, watching everything that was taking place, unconscious of Marlingham's tight grip on her shoulders.

Meanwhile, Jefferson was grinding his pelvis into the bucking girl beneath him as she arched her back and thrust upward so that they were banging and slamming into each other with powerful force. Her mouth was open and her head flailed from side to side in savage abandon.

"Fuck me! Harder! Harder!" she moaned deliriously. "Stick your finger in my ass, hard!"

Thrusting his hand between her melon-round buttocks, he insinuated his middle finger into her anus, driving it into the tight, rubbery ring until it entered with a popping sound. He pushed hard until it began to glide in smoothly, and her buttocks

churned and bounced up and down off the table. Gritting his teeth, he sank it in deeper up to the second knuckle, bringing a wild shriek from her throat.

"Aaa! Ooo! Go on, hurt me!" she begged, revelling in the dual skewering of her body. Her ass-cheeks pumped down until they were buried in the palm of his hand. Rotating his finger inside the hot, spongy depths of her rectum, he felt her muscles spasming around it, and then he withdrew it, only to shove it in deep once again, bringing another moan from her throat. His wetly glistening penis continued to saw in and out, rippling deep in the velvety passage of her cunt chamber, matched by the rhythm of his finger skewering her ass. To his delight she was moving faster and faster, bucking her loins up and down, opening and closing her legs around his hips.

He could tell she was nearing climax for she began to groan and grunt wildly, her heels kicking down on his back, her head twisting and squirming on the laboratory table. She was gurgling and gasping, and, overcome with savage desire, he fucked his finger in and out of her tight little anal hole while his cock screwed mercilessly up into the rippling depths of her pussy.

"Oooh, unnghh! I'm coming!" Jennifer gasped frantically. "Fuck me harder, harder!"

She drew her thighs back further until the whole of her wide-stretched pussy was offered up to him to do with as he pleased. Her legs locked around his back and her pelvis writhed and jerked in a dance of abandoned desire. Her eyes rolled up toward the ceiling, her nostrils flared as she desperately gasped for air. They were both too involved to notice the door of the adjoining staff room being pushed open wider and the two faces that were peering out from the opening, one frozen in horror, the other set with a smug smile of sadistic glee.

A low, muffled scream suddenly forced itself from between the female researcher's lips and she screwed herself up on Jefferson's long, thick cock, locking his body tightly to hers as she jerked and spasmed with uncontrollable delight. A moment later she collapsed backwards, her legs dropping limply from her partner's body. She lay still except for a spasmodic trembling of her thighs as her cunt lips clasped loosely around his cock. Once again he thrust deep into her till he came, but he knew that she was already satisfied and besides, when she managed to rouse herself once again it would be even better. Jesus, she was incredible! He had never been so excited by anyone before in his life. She was the kind of woman he'd only dreamed about and lusted after in his secret imagination, but now all his fantasies had come true in the unlikeliest of places.

"Ummmh, that was nice," she moaned, coming to. "Your cock was so hard. It's still hard, isn't it?"

"Damn, you're not kidding," he groaned down at her despite the throbbing ache in his sperm-bloated testicles.

"Well, I'll have to do something about that. Lie down next to me."

Without protesting, he did what she ordered, stretching out on his back. Hell, he might as well let her have her way, since she'd managed things pretty well up to this point. He could see her crawling over toward him as his rigid member pointed straight up toward the ceiling like a rocket on a launching pad. He folded his arms under his head so he could watch as she reached out and began stroking him, sliding the loose outer shaft of his penis up and down in a mesmerising rhythm that sent throbs of pleasure down through his balls. Quickly, she drew herself up on her knees and leaned over his loins, her seductive face only a few inches away from his stiffly bulging penis, her long, black hair grazing his thighs and stomach.

Slowly, her head lowered and her tongue flicked teasingly into the wet, tiny opening of the tip. Groaning, he sucked in his breath as chills rippled up his spine and she dipped lower, enveloping the blood-engorged head between her soft, warm lips. As her hungry mouth tightened, he jerked his hips upward, pushing the thick rod of wet flesh deeper inside her.

"Jesus, that's good," he gasped, raising his head up slightly for a clearer view of her contorted face. The lewdly exciting sight of his glistening cock embedded halfway in her mouth sent sparks of pleasure rippling all over his body. It gleamed in the semi-darkness of the room, matching the gleams of her glistening lips as they nibbled around it. Jesus, it was like a crazy dream. He felt her massaging the soft, bloated skin of his balls tantalisingly with one hand while the thumb and forefinger of the other stroked its thick, blue-veined base as she began to suck rhythmically up and down. He could feel the velvety softness of her tongue twirling maddeningly around it each time she withdrew her head, the tip flicking teasingly across the tiny split of the glans. He flexed his buttocks, his head still lifted up, his neck straining and his eyes focused on her bobbing head.

Jennifer Wilson, for her part, sensed her partner's throbbing reaction and began to suck harder, the tips of her teeth nibbling at the bulging flesh that burgeoned inside her mouth, and she reached under his buttocks to pull his loins tighter up against her mouth.

Her tongue swiped around the membrane on the underside of his cock until he felt it swelling almost to the bursting point. His eyes widened as he watched her taking the fleshy organ further and further down her throat without choking. By God, she really knew what she was doing! She was giving him more pleasure than he ever thought possible.

A furnace of heat began to glow in the depths of his cum-bloated balls as he watched her lust-contorted face working over his wildly jerking cock. Tiny streams of sweat rolled down the girl's naked body as she bucked over him like a demon gone insane. The muscles of his stomach tightened like steel rods until he felt as though they were going to snap, and he arched his back up, shoving his penis even deeper into her throat, her lips hungrily clasping and sucking at it.

He gasped suddenly, the moment of orgasm arriving. A low, guttural moan came from somewhere deep in his chest as he felt streams of white-hot cum jerking from the tip of his cock into her eagerly sucking mouth. Her cheeks puffed and hollowed as she greedily swallowed the warm gushes of fiery liquid, her Adam's apple bobbing up and down with fierce quickness. His fingers tangled savagely in her hair, holding her head tight against his loins as he rammed his hotly jerking flesh against her tonsils.

Finally he moaned and with a long sigh fell flat on his back once again on the cold marble table, his cock gradually deflating like a balloon with the air escaping from it. But she continued to gently nibble and suck him, drawing every last ounce of white fluid from his penis, licking hungrily the reddened tip of his cock. At last it was over, and she crawled up over him, nestling her head against his, planting kisses on the length of his neck.

"That was nice, wasn't it?" she murmured. "We can do more of it. This isn't the last time."

"Ummhhh," he groaned in reply, unable to say anything else. His body was sated and relaxed, and he could only look into her eyes with a grateful expression of pleasure on his face. Jesus, he'd never realised it could be this good.

"There's more we can do," she said softly. "Much more."

He propped himself up on his elbows and nervously searched the lab with his eyes.

"Did you hear something?"

"No, darling. Don't be ridiculous. It's nothing."

Chapter 6

Stephen Marlingham had managed to put on a good act of indignation as he remained at the door with Catherine Peterson, watching the two lewdly coupled bodies grind their way toward orgasm. But still an inward sadistic satisfaction filled him as he observed the horrified expression on the young wife's face, and his cock jerked beneath his trousers under the influence of the salacious scene. It bulged even harder when Catherine backed into his arms, recoiling from what she'd witnessed.

Though he would have liked nothing more than to grab her just then and throw her down on one of the long couches in the staff room, he knew she was not ripe yet. She was still in a state of shock, and he had to bide his time until she recovered, reverting back to the relative coolness of smouldering anger. There was nothing a woman seeking vengeance wouldn't do, no matter how puritanical she might be under normal conditions.

This was something he'd learned a long time ago and had used to draw other inexperienced couples into the group to do what they jokingly called extracurricular scientific research. Practically three-quarters of the staff were in the game now, and Marlingham would have liked nothing more than to bring Catherine and Jefferson in too. Hell, she seemed so naïve and virginal he would just love to sink his cock deep inside her pussy.

He had to admit, of course, that Jennifer Wilson had certainly helped matters along. Ever since Peterson had joined the Centre, she'd had hot pants for him, and Jennifer wasn't one who could be stopped easily. She'd gone after Peterson with all the ardour of a bitch on heat. She wasn't the only one, though. Practically everyone in the place had their eyes set on the newcomers. And with Jennifer doing her job, it was going to be easy for him to sink his claws into Peterson's young redheaded wife. Everything had been moving along smoothly – the job for Catherine, Jennifer's efforts to seduce her husband, and now finally the brutal confrontation, which, while it wasn't exactly staged, had fallen neatly into place – beautifully, in fact, considering this was Catherine's first day on the job. It meant he wouldn't have to spend days and days softening her up. The sight of her husband screwing Jennifer Wilson had done the job for him.

Damn, he thought to himself, he was going to have a hell of a good time this evening. The proud, innocent type had always presented a challenge to him, and he liked nothing more than to see them fall under the spell of his thick, bulging cock in a state of helpless submission. Later, once he'd completed her initiation, so to speak, he would turn her over to the rest of the club, which included some colourful townspeople as well as the scientists and their wives. She would know she'd really been fucked when he had finished with her.

"Well, your husband really went at it with a lot of gusto," Marlingham said, trying to preserve at the same time an air of dignity.

"That bastard," she hissed viciously. "How could he do something like this to me?"

It was the right moment, Marlingham realised, because she was filled with anger now, and so he jerked her head toward his and pressed his lips hotly against hers, eagerly working his tongue into her mouth. She groaned and tried to squirm away, but suddenly he released his grip on her shoulder.

"That was just to calm you down," he said, staring into her eyes. "You wouldn't want to do anything rash, would you, like breaking in there?"

She could see he was right, though he had a strange way of proving it. Nevertheless, she tried to loose the tenseness in her muscles, though Marlingham's sudden kiss had made her more disconcerted than ever. It was the first time another man had kissed her since her marriage, and to her surprise, her body had responded to it. It was exciting, and it even seemed natural, even though she knew it was wrong. In spite of her confusion, she had felt tiny ripples of pleasure running through her stomach. But what would happen now? She was so terribly distraught she didn't know where to turn for comfort.

She cast her gaze downward and pressed the back of her hand to her mouth in an effort to control the powerful emotions that were welling inside her. She had never imagined that she would be kissed by another man, and she didn't have the slightest idea about what to do next. Her mind told her to run, but where? She didn't have a home any more, couldn't have a home after she'd witnessed what her husband had done, but there was nowhere else to turn but to the protective warmth of Stephen Marlingham's arms. Yes, he had helped her, and she was grateful for it. Without him, she might well have suffered a nervous breakdown witnessing the scene between her husband and the licentious woman who had obviously seduced him. Thank God, the worst was over now, but the two bodies were still nakedly entwined on the lab table, and she couldn't take her eyes off them. She hardly dared breathe for fear of disturbing the scene and making her presence known.

"She sucked him off," Marlingham whispered in her ear, pulling her more tightly against him and grinding his hips ever so slowly against her ass as they resumed their watching position, peering through the crack in the half-opened doorway.

She spun around and faced him once again, burying her head in his chest.

"Oh God, it was terrible." She tried to remain strong, but once again the tears were flowing freely from her eyes. The horrible sight of her husband's penis disappearing deep inside the other woman's mouth was too much for her to bear, and sobs wracked her body. Echoes of the terrible groaning and sucking sounds they had made flooded her ears, even though the event had passed moments ago. In her imagination it was still going on. It was too horribly real to deny! The mewls, the groans, the leathery bucking noises of flesh against naked flesh assaulted her mind, driving her to the point of insanity. Her own husband had been doing all this, had been enjoying every second of it as she watched unbeknownst to him. It was like a frightening nightmare, and desperately she wanted to escape from it. She wanted to run away but knew that her legs wouldn't support her, and the only alternative was to remain supported in Marlingham's arms, listening while her husband and the strange woman exchanged secretive whispers as they embraced each other.

Suddenly she realised that the director's hands had crept up on her and were massaging one of her breasts. He gave a quick, sharp pinch against her nipple that brought a gasp from her throat as her body tensed in instinctive reaction. A flash of pain shot down the length of her spine and she twisted in his arms in an effort to break away. Her mind was a mess of the sights and sounds she had experienced during the day. She was practically hallucinating as she saw naked arms and legs twisting around each other, bellies thudding against bellies, and stiff penises penetrating the depths of wet, welcoming vaginas. But it was no dream, it was real; she had seen it all, and her husband had been a participant in the lewd goings-on.

At the same time that she was repulsed by these salacious images, she couldn't help feeling ripples of pleasure flowing through her belly as the older scientist squeezed and kneaded her breasts. She clenched her eyes shut, but the feelings wouldn't go away as Marlingham manipulated her and began to undo the buttons of her blouse.

In protest, she uttered a low helpless

groan, which was quickly cut off by the older man's lips pressing against hers, his tongue gliding warmly into her mouth and snaking against the backs of her teeth. She tried to get away, but his strength was overpowering, and her movements only seemed to incite him more so that he crushed her body even tighter against his. If she struggled too much, she would only make her presence known to her husband and the other woman, and that she didn't want to do at any cost. If he caught her the way she was now, she would never be able to vent her anger. She would only be laughed at. After all, she hadn't chosen what was happening now, she had been forced into it.

"Did you see it all?" Marlingham whispered in her ear. "He licked her cunt and then she sucked his cock."

"Y-yes, I saw it," she mumbled in reply, the lewd words stimulating something deep inside her body.

"You're not going to let him get away with it, are you? You've got to pay him back." As the words escaped from his mouth he pulled her around so that they were facing each other and ground his pelvis tightly against hers. He dug his hands into the softness of her buttocks and squeezed them rhythmically until he could feel her cunt pressing against his throbbing, confined cock.

"N-no, please. We can't! We can't do this!" she whimpered helplessly.

"Sure we can," he said grinning. "We're just going to make things even." His voice sounded harsh, even cruel, and suddenly he locked his mouth tight against hers, spearing his tongue deep inside her throat.

"Please, God, no! Don't do this!" she begged, struggling, trying to tear herself away. But it was futile, and she knew that he had the upper hand. Oh God! Why hadn't she listened to Jefferson when he'd told her not to take this job? It would destroy both of them!

Her body tensed as Marlingham began to squeeze and knead her soft ass-cheeks through the material of her skirt, pulling her loins hard against him until she thought she couldn't bear the pressure any longer. She clenched her eyes shut, fighting with her mind against the involuntary sensations of excited pleasure that were sweeping through her body. The soft, tingling touch of his fingers against her nipples, however, was too much, and she felt herself falling slowly, ever so slowly into submission.

"Ummmh, you're fantastic," the older man groaned throatily. "You're going to enjoy this, believe me, you will."

"No," she pleaded, trying to dissuade him. "No one but my husband has ever touched me."

"You've been missing something then. Don't worry, the experience will do you good."

He slipped his hand between her breasts and over the smooth surface of her belly as Catherine gasped and held her breath. She felt his fingers on the hem of her skirt slowly raising it up to the tops of her thighs. His fingers suddenly touched against her naked flesh, and she squirmed back with a helpless whimper as one fingertip glided slowly under the legband of her panties, making sudden wet contact with the sensitive tip of her clitoris. Gently pushing aside the nest of soft, red pubic hair, he dipped his middle finger into the wetly trembling passage of Catherine's hotly aroused cunt. It was damp and slippery from the effects of unwanted desire that had pervaded her as she witnessed the scene in the adjacent lab. She held her breath to contain the groan of helpless pleasure that was welling inside her and desperately needed to be expressed. She knew she couldn't make a sound now or else her husband would be attracted, and he would discover her in Marlingham's lewd embrace. As she found herself reacting to the older man's skilful ministrations, tears of humiliation flowed down her cheeks, but her shame did not contain the instinctive movements of her loins. She squirmed her hips, in spite of all the efforts to control herself, against his rummaging fingers.

"Spread them wider," he breathed fervently in her ear, "good and wide. You love it, you know you do."

"G-god, please. Don't make me do this," she begged piteously. "Jefferson will see us, I'm sure of it!"

"Let's go somewhere else then. Come on, what do you say?" he asked once more as his finger glided in and out of her rhythmically clasping cunt.

"Yes, anything," she murmured. "Please, take me away from here."

Reaching behind her, she grasped the doorknob and pulled the door carefully shut as though to block out from her memory all the horrible scenes she had witnessed taking place. When the door clicked she suddenly felt free, strange hallucinatory sensations dancing in her mind. Somewhere in the back of her head she knew she had said something wrong, but it was too late to do anything else. The strong sensations in her body had run away with her, and she was no longer free to follow the dictates of her own conscience.

He grasped her hand powerfully and led her out through the lounge, along the dimly lit corridors and to the elevator, pressing the button for the third floor.

"Where are we going?" she asked, her mind a bog of hopeless confusion.

"Don't worry, you'll see. You want to get back at him, don't you?"

Nothing made sense now, she thought; she was somewhere in a dream world, and she responded mechanically.

"Yes, yes, I want to get back at him."

"Good, I'm going to help you then."

Yes, he was going to help her. He was such a kind man. He had helped her already, consoled her when she had seen what was happening in the lab this morning. But still she remembered what Jefferson had told her. He's a lecher. He'll chase you around his desk. She remembered his hands squeezing her breasts, his mouth pressing down hard on hers and his tongue slipping between her teeth. She was so totally confused she didn't know what to do. She could only submit to the influence of someone stronger than she, which she did now as he led her out of the elevator once it had reached the third floor.

He grasped her by the hand and led her to a locked door, fumbling in his pocket for the key. As he did so, a raging anger welled inside her. How dare her husband cheat on her? How dare he fuck that strange woman? They'd only been married six months and already he was dissatisfied with her. She hated him! Her loathing was so great she would do anything for revenge.

The door swung open and Marlingham led her into an elegantly furnished room, with thick, plush carpeting, wood cabinets and white leather sofas.

"This is the boardroom," he informed her. "You're a lucky girl. It's not everyone who gets to see the boardroom on their first day at work."

"Yes," she whispered. "I have to sit down."

Mechanically she directed herself to one of the sofas and flopped down on it, a dazed look in her eyes as the director stood over her, a grin of conquest sweeping over his face. Suddenly, he was sitting next to her, his arms around her shoulders, drawing her close to his body as his lips pressed against hers, and he kissed her with fiery passion. She could feel the hardness of his pulsating penis digging into the soft flesh of her upper thighs, but made no move to protest.

In her state of desperate misery she tried not to think as his hands glided down the front of her blouse, carefully undoing the buttons and spreading it wide. The snaps of her brassiere came next, and she heard him sigh in lewd appreciation as it came loose to reveal her white, trembling breasts. He slipped the blouse and brassiere off her until the entire top half was completely naked, and she gazed at him in dazed wonderment. What was happening to her? She was in a state of shock and barely knew what she was doing. A second later she heard the faint whizzing sound of a zipper and then saw him wriggling her skirt down off her hips and jerking it free from her ankles. Then he was down on his knees in front of her, drawing her panties down over the smooth, white curves of her buttocks. He tugged them loose, and they too landed with the pile of other discarded clothing.

She was totally naked, completely at his mercy, and he gazed at her with leering eyes, his tongue flicking across his lower lip in lewd appreciation of her body. Suddenly he pressed forward, his lips caressing her belly, his tongue flicking into her navel in a tantalising rhythm. She lay back against the cushions, and her arms involuntarily reached out, locking into his thick, prematurely grey hair.

Her husband had cheated on her. She had watched him as he sucked another woman's vagina and as the woman had sucked his cock in return. She was free now, free to wreak her vengeance on him, and she was going to do it any way she could. It was obscene, lewd, what her husband had done, and at that very moment, without her fully realising it, the director was doing the same thing her husband had performed on the dark-haired woman. His lips had dropped to her vagina, and his tongue was suddenly wriggling in between her cunt-lips, making her squirm and jerk in a mad frenzy.

"S-stop, please! No, don't do that," Catherine stammered, trying to push him away, but it was totally useless as he grasped the backs of her thighs and levered them high and wide in the air. Suddenly he began grunting and mewling like an animal, his teeth chopping into the downy fringe of her cunt hairs as his tongue speared into her involuntarily quivering pussy.

"No, don't do this to me," the young wife begged. "Oh God, no! Please take your tongue out of there."

She jerked at his head and squeezed her legs around his neck in a vice-like scissors grip, but nothing happened. It all seemed to excite him more. He was lapping wetly at her cunt like an excited animal, the forefinger of each hand worming toward the crevice between her buttocks.

Oh God, she thought. I'm doing the same thing that vile woman was doing with my husband, and I can't help myself. There's no escape. It's so lewd! The older man's wetly licking tongue was spearing in and out of her, mining the hot liquid of her vaginal passage as it slithered up inside her like a jungle snake.

"No, don't suck me! Please don't suck me!" she groaned desperately, trying to squirm loose from his grip. But his fingers were clawing into her naked flesh; he was dragging her loins tighter and tighter against his mouth; his tongue was sinking even deeper. She was going insane. She wanted to scream and yet she couldn't break away, for somewhere deep inside, she was actually enjoying herself. She was enjoying the lewd, vile licking of her loins.

Her legs spread wider until they formed a giant vee, her feet pointing upward at the ceiling. His head bobbed frantically in and out, moaning, mewling noises coming from his throat all the while. Her wetly throbbing cunt-lips clasped and unclasped hungrily around his tongue, and she knew she was lost now. The last faint voice of her conscience pleaded with her, but it was growing dimmer and dimmer inside.

"No, no, it's not right. No, don't kiss me there," the young redheaded wife mumbled, but her breath was coming heavily and her heart beating madly inside her throat. As she squirmed and bucked against his lewd tongue-fucking, his middle finger suddenly rammed up into her tightly puckering anus and she lurched with spasmodic pain.

At the same time, her buttocks churned and ground down on them as though her body were completely at war with her mind. No, this couldn't be happening; she would never do anything like this, and yet she knew it wasn't a dream. She was being obscenely abused by this older man and actually enjoying it, though she couldn't yet fully admit it to herself. Suddenly, he withdrew his fingers and gripped her buttocks with a powerful force and hoisted her over his shoulders as she kicked and squirmed in protest. Bending low, he set her down on the thickly carpeted floor, pinning her shoulders in place and grinning at her like a sadistic beast that had quarried its prey.

"Oh God, you can't do this," she protested weakly, clenching her eyes tightly shut as though to block out the horror of what was going to happen.

"Don't worry, baby. I'm going to, no matter what you say."

Her whole body trembled as she imagined what was going to happen to her next, but it was not a simple trembling of fear. There was a tense enjoyment in it, too, though she still couldn't admit it to herself.

"Just relax, baby," he crooned. "There's no way you can fight me off. So just relax and enjoy it. I'm gonna plant my cock inside that sweet little pussy of yours. You'll never be the same again. But first I'm gonna finish where I left off."

Catherine knew exactly what he meant, and while she made a feeble effort to close her legs, her body refused to respond to the commands of her mind. Raising her head, she watched in horror as he licked his lips to continue the unceremonious tongue-fucking of her cunt which he'd begun only moments ago.

"Ready?" he said, grinning down at her. "Ready or not, here I come."

Catherine groaned in helpless submission as her body trembled with suppressed desire. She didn't know if she could resist any longer. His skilful tongue inside her vagina might turn her into a raving whore any minute, but there was no choice. She could only do what he wanted.

"I'm going to suck it now, baby. I'm gonna really suck it this time," he growled at her, his powerful hands massaging the insides of her thighs.

Suddenly his head lunged at the triangle of her loins and his tongue rammed deep up inside her pussy, even deeper than it had gone before.

"Oh God! Ooohhh!" she gasped, twitching uncontrollably as he flicked out against the tiny bud of her clitoris then drew back through the exposed sensitive flesh of her helplessly dilating cunt. As his mouth and tongue worked feverishly over the widespread tightness of her pussy, her eyes opened and she gazed down at his bobbing head. She could see him grinning in the throes of lewd conquest as she groaned from deep in her chest with each maddening thrust of his tongue, probing the depths of her cunt walls.

It slipped up and down inside her and then withdrew as he bent his head lower to lick the inner flesh of her anal crevice, sending spasms of lewd pleasure up her spine. He levered her knees back until her kneecaps rubbed against her breasts, exposing her ravaged loins even more fully to his eager mouth and tongue.

He flicked into her cunt harder and faster with his tongue as her incomprehensible whimpers flooded the room with the music of abandoned lust. His body and mind inflamed with carnal desire, he flicked his tongue into her tight anal ring, making her jerk and mewl at the unexpected contact. She was beyond hope now, her shamelessly aroused body having deserted her. There was nothing she could do but yield herself to the perverted desires of this powerful older man who was debasing her with no thought of pity or compassion.

Rhythmically she thrust her cunt up

toward his face, arching her back as she did so. She groaned as he responded with a stab of his tongue, his teeth clamping tightly down on her vaginal mound. Her body quivered and bucked beneath the overpowering assault, and her stomach churned with the incredible pleasures of naked sexual abandon.

Sensing her ultimate surrender, Marlingham, with a savage grin on his face, thrust his thick, wet tongue even deeper inside her quivering cunt-sheath and felt her soft, silky pubic hairs graze against the tip of his nose as she ground her buttocks ecstatically up against him. He felt her vaginal lips twitching around his tongue as they opened and closed spasmodically, as though to milk it like a cock. She was one hell of a whore after she got her motor running, he reasoned to himself.

Her helplessly aroused body writhed and squirmed shamelessly against the deep, probing tongue of the director until she thought she would go insane from the lewd licking of her loins. She arched upward from her hips and grasped his hair, tangling her fingers tightly into it and pressing his head even harder against her wildly palpitating pussy, a low soul-stirring moan escaping from her lips. Nothing mattered any more but the wild pleasure of his boring tongue steaming in and out between her cunt lips. She loved it, she wanted it and yet she knew it was wrong. Her head fell back, her hair dangling loosely over her shoulders as she crooned and chanted a litany of salacious abandon. Her lips bared back over her gleaming white teeth and the cords of her neck stood out like steel rods as she strained to pump every last ounce of pleasure from the punishing lash of his tongue.

"Aaagggh, ugggh, God! I'm coming!" she sputtered, her face contorted in a mask of lust.

She trembled and shook, her legs flapping and spasming as the older man relentlessly glided his tongue in and out of the secret recesses of her body. Her body shuddered and suddenly hot waves of cum flooded out from deeper inside her womb, pouring in a sweet flood over his hungrily sucking mouth and dribbling down the insides of her quivering thighs. The room seemed to cave in on the young wife with a great reverberating crash, and she gasped and moaned as he sucked and burrowed between her thighs, which were locked around his neck. Slowly her fingers untwined from his tousled hair, and she released her grip, allowing him to withdraw his head.

Marlingham pulled himself up to a standing position until he was looming over her, staring down the length of her sweat-streaked body as the juices of her orgasm masked his mouth and lips, making them glisten lewdly in the dim light of the curtained room. Catherine closed her eyes tightly in an effort to blot out the sight of him and the memory of the degrading, humiliating things they'd just done. The shame of her own weakness and submission brought her back to reality but it was Marlingham who spoke first.

"We're not finished yet," he said with a cruel triumphant smile on his face. "You haven't paid your husband back completely."

"W-what are you going to do?" her voice quavered.

"Now I'm going to fuck you, Catherine. Fuck you like you've never had it before."

His crude words sent a new flurry of excitement rippling through her still-aroused loins and suppressed the shame and humiliation that nagged her. Suddenly, she flushed with anger, not at Marlingham but at her husband, for she could still see in her mind his penis buried in the other woman's secret flesh up to the hilt, a pleased expression on his face. He had enjoyed what he'd done, and now Catherine was determined to enjoy herself as well, no matter how obscene and degrading her conscience told her it was.

"Yes, Stephen, fuck me. Yes. Stick your penis in between my legs," she suddenly begged him, her eyes frozen in hard determination.

She did not have to urge him on any longer, for immediately he had stripped off his clothes and was crawling in between her lewdly splayed legs, his thick, rigid penis jutting out large and throbbing, his heavily swaying balls swollen with sperm that was going to rocket deep up into the depths of her belly. If only Jefferson could see her now, it would teach him the lesson of his life. You bastard, you adulterer, she cursed inwardly at him.

Chapter 7

The light in the laboratory was growing dim as afternoon faded into evening. Jefferson was half-dressed now but still incredibly horny, his cock bulging and throbbing as it came to life again.

"Hmm, I can see you're still going strong," Jennifer whispered, jerking down his shorts before he had a chance to zip up his trousers. Her fingers curled lightly around the swollen head and she began massaging it until the ache in his balls was almost unbearable.

"Damn, I want to screw you again," he said, smiling at her, his body charged with excitement. "But can't we find somewhere else?"

"You mean some place more comfortable? I think I know just where. But we'll both have to get dressed to get there. Are you sure you can walk through the corridors with your cock that stiff?"

"Jesus, it's gonna break through my pants," he moaned, but wasting no time, Jennifer grasped him by the wrist and led him out from the lab to the elevator.

"Where are we going?" he asked.

"To the boardroom on the third floor."

"How in the world will we get in? It's locked, isn't it?"

"Don't worry about that. I have the key. I've got connections."

The ride up in the elevator, though it took less than a minute, seemed interminable to the young scientist. His cock and balls were aching as though they'd been slugged by a sledgehammer, and he could barely wait to screw the dark-haired temptress beside him once again. Jesus, he wondered how much of this kind of thing went on at the Centre, because he'd certainly gotten a strong impression that he and Jennifer weren't the first ones to have a little fun experimenting in biology.

As the elevator stopped and Jennifer led him out, he felt like a misbehaving schoolboy, stimulated by the thought of sneaking about and the possibility of being caught. My God, Catherine would never forgive him, and he'd be disgraced. He'd have to get a job somewhere teaching high school biology... his career would be ruined, but at the moment nothing mattered except the thought of putting his cock into his sultry seductress one more time. He glanced down the corridor both ways in front of the boardroom door and, seeing it was all clear, motioned to Jennifer to put the key in the lock.

"Listen," she said, as she put her ear to the door. "There's someone inside there."

There was all right, and he knew damn well what they were doing. Moaning, gasping noises were coming from the room, the sounds of a grappling struggle going on. A man and woman were inside there, but who were they? This strange place was getting more and more interesting by the minute, Jefferson told himself.

"Take a look at it," the male voice said. "I want you to see how big it is. Open your eyes, come on!"

"Jesus Christ, it's Marlingham!" Jefferson whispered hoarsely. "He's in there screwing somebody."

"Shh," Jennifer whispered. "We can go around the balcony and look through the windows."

"W-wait a minute. I don't know whether we should or not."

"Don't be silly. This'll be fun. I think he's got somebody new."

Jefferson knew he was taking a crazy chance but didn't resist as Jennifer grasped his hand and led him through an adjacent room to the balcony and slowly toward the French windows looking in on the boardroom. He had to admit that the sight of the director balling a young, nubile chick would turn him on no end, though he wondered how long he'd be able to stand the tease.

* * *

Catherine finally opened her eyes at the director's prodding and focused on the mammoth penis about to penetrate her vagina. It was huge and pulsing like an animal, thick and spear-tipped, with one pearl of pre-ejaculate glistening on the lust-bloated cock-head. He was torturing her, making her gaze at it like this, and she wondered how her tight cunt opening could ever stretch wide enough to handle its thick shaft... oh God! It would split her in half.

"That was just a teaser. Now I'm gonna ram it inside you, baby. I'm gonna ram it all the way up to your mouth."

Catherine felt her body soiled and debased

and desperately wished she had the presence of mind to escape, but in spite of her horror she was frozen in fascination. The thick cock mesmerised her, and in spite of its awesome size, she craved it deep inside her throbbing loins.

He moved forward slowly, menacingly, on his knees, aiming for her flowering cunt-slit which he had already widened slightly with his tongue-fucking. Staring directly into the young wife's frightened eyes, he grinned in triumph as he began stroking the heavy, uncircumcised foreskin back and forth over the hard, bulbously swollen head.

"Do you think you can take all this?" he said, grinning, an obscene gleam burning in his eyes.

Catherine found the words freezing inside her mouth and she sucked her breath in. Her eyes fixed on the powerfully built body of her husband's superior, then lowered once more to the swollen, fleshy instrument he held in his hands. Oh God, it was huge, like a heavy but flexible club. She had always thought her husband's penis was big, but this... it would split her apart and burst through her cervix. She tried to envision it buried inside the tight walls of her vagina, and a quiver of cold fear streaked down her spine.

"It's... it's too big," she stammered helplessly as he continued to massage it teasingly only inches away from her palpitating, eager cunt-lips.

"It's just right," he said. "It'll loosen you up inside. That's what you need, my dear, a little loosening up."

Bending forward over her naked, trembling body, he suddenly fastened his teeth on the nipple of her left breast, bringing a yelp of pain from her lips. She groaned, twisting her head to one side, and attempted to squirm free, but his hand pressed down on her hips, pinning her tight against the cool leather sofa. His lips hungrily explored the white, trembling mounds, sending a blissful twitch coursing down to her loins. Her naked buttocks began to move.

"Goddamn, I'm going to fuck you," he gloated. "I'm going to ram it in so deep you'll be crying for me. I'm gonna stretch that tight little pussy as wide as it'll go."

Catherine shuddered under the prodding of his obscene words. She could feel the bulging hugeness of his penis brush against her thigh, and she reached down eagerly to grasp it, forcing all thought of wrongdoing from her tortured mind.

The director moved up over the rapidly panting young girl, grinning broadly as he felt her fingers grip his stiff, aching flesh and tug on it until it bulged even wider. He felt her trembling in fear and joy at its enormous size, realising she had never seen or handled anything like it before in her life. Her muscles tensed as she braced her body and then guided it up the crevice between her buttocks, holding it tight to her flesh until it was poised against the wetly gaping lips of her hungry cunt-mouth. Quivering half in fear and half in anticipation, she glided her thighs wide apart and placed her trembling hands on his ass-cheeks, awaiting the first hot, hard thrust of his enormous male shaft. She felt the hot, spongy head moving slowly up and down, parting her pubic hair and fleshy pussy lips, then all of a sudden, her tight cunt-mouth flowered open as though by magic command.

"Aaaauuuuu!" she grunted as the elastic-rimmed tightness gave way and the burgeoning tip slipped through, cruelly stretching the tight opening until she felt as though her body would rip in half from the savage pressure.

A sadistic wave of pleasure raced through Marlingham as her soulful protest came to his ears. His face twisted itself into a vicious mask of lust, his lips formed a cruel smile and he thrust a little harder, bringing another long, low moan from her throat.

"N-n-no. No! Aaaagh, it hurts!" the young redheaded bride whimpered piteously as the director drove another agonising inch up into her wetly fevered vagina. God, he was too big! He was going to tear out her insides.

Stephen Marlingham's body was on fire with the excitement her anguished pleas were bringing him as he slowly and relentlessly penetrated her hot little cunt, flexing his hips slowly and excruciatingly sinking up into her belly an inch at a time. His face was red and a light film of perspiration coated his forehead as he strained to go even deeper into her tightly clasping pussy. Goddamn, he had to fuck the little bitch. Now! He couldn't wait a second longer.

Ramming forward without mercy, he dropped his heavy weight down on her, smashing her full, stiff-nippled tits tight against her chest, thrusting his hips quickly and plunging his long, throbbing cock in her moistly trembling cunt with the savage force of a battering ram. The warm, moist flesh of vaginal walls rippled in velvety waves before him, and his sperm-bloated balls slapped against her nakedly upturned ass-cheeks with a leather thud.

"Oh no, oh no, please stop!" she breathed in agony. "You're killing me." Her legs, splayed wide apart, flailed frantically in the air on either side of his massive body as her pelvis bucked and jerked against his weight. Her arms pushed against his pulsing hips, trying to keep his stiff rod of flesh from penetrating any further into her belly, but it was a futile effort as he rammed into her like an incensed bull.

Her belly was on the verge of exploding from the thick, pulsating organ that filled and expanded inside it, and his long, rigid penis was ripping her insides to shreds. She could feel every fleshy ridge cruelly stretching her apart as it throbbed inside her. When she moaned in protest and bucked against this carnal onslaught she felt him beginning to move harder and faster. Sucking in her breath, she held it until she was afraid that her chest would burst. His hips and buttocks flexed and within seconds he had established a powerful in-and-out fucking tempo which rocked her naked, twisting body.

The young wife flexed her vaginal sphincter tightly in an effort to trap the huge, invading bludgeon, but the throb of her internal sinews only seemed to excite him more, so that the ramming thrusts of his long, hard penis continued to punish her without mercy. Helplessly she clenched her teeth and kept her eyes tightly shut, her muscles straining, her heart pounding frenziedly in her chest. The vengeance was his now and not hers, for she realised she was no better than her husband, letting herself submit to this brutal ravishment of her loins. She knew she would never be the same again. She was a whore, a cheap slut, because in spite of the pangs of conscience that still pierced her, she was actually enjoying herself and could not stop the salacious act being performed on her body. There was nothing left to her but the thick, punishing penis that sawed viciously in and out of her vaginal flesh.

Marlingham sensed her resistance falling to the wayside and knew it wouldn't take much more to turn this soft-bodied young wife into a squealing mass of raving desire. Even though she'd fought him at the beginning he had always sensed the passionate streak behind her mask of righteousness and knew that he could turn her into a lust-crazed slut. They all came around, he had said before, and she was living up to his previous experiences. Damn, she would make a hell of a nice addition to the little club, and after this she couldn't very well refuse.

Catherine, for her part, was beginning to feel licentious tingles of lewd desire spreading all through her body, chills creeping up and down her spine to the rhythm of Marlingham's powerful hips jerking as he pushed his cock up into the secret regions of her inner loins. Her body was squirming and writhing of its own will as she groaned frantically into his mouth, shoving her tongue with rhythmic abandon into his throat, mingling their salivas in a pool of sensual liquid. Desperate to take him even further inside, she drew back her legs, spreading her hungrily gaping pussy even wider to his battering assault, her naked, rounded buttocks grinding and pumping upward as she chanted a rhythmic incantation, her muscles straining, her teeth grinding savagely together.

Marlingham ran his hands down her smoothly curved flanks and slid them under the trembling globes of her buttocks, digging his fingernails into the softly yielding flesh. They were flexing and unflexing, oozing like dough, palpitating in his fingers as he dug harder and harder into them. With a grunt he jerked her tight little pussy up tighter to his loins and felt her thighs straining further back, the moistly throbbing hole of her pussy expanding even wider to greet each relentless thrust.

Catherine did not even try to figure out what had happened to her. All she wanted now was to feel the crazed wave of lustful arousal that had possessed her from head to toe and saturated her whole being. She knew only that the initial pain had given way to sensations of joy that she'd never experienced in her life, even when her husband had fucked her. This was something new and exciting, and her body had completely surrendered to it. Electric-like tingles that began deep within her womb pulsed outward to all parts of her body, even to the farthest reaches of her fingertips. Her eyes clenched tightly shut and she worked her tongue deep into his slavering mouth as small, intense mewls of desperate pleasure escaped from her lips. The muscles in her body worked and rippled, the veins in her neck stood out in intense relief, and she writhed and ground her pelvis to suck his cock for everything it was worth. Her mind had deserted her, and the sensual pleasures of the body had taken over completely. It didn't matter who was fucking her. The only thing that mattered was the hard, stiff cock that was driving deeper and deeper into her pussy, making sucking, sluicing noises with each demonic thrust.

The lecherous grin on Marlingham's face widened as the young, naked body crushed beneath him increased the tempo of its hungry up-and-down gyrations. The shamelessly aroused redheaded bride moved faster and faster with each fleeting second, pumping her hot little cunt up and down on his thickened penis as though to signal the urgency of her desire. He could see that she had completely transformed herself into a savage nymphomaniac, her teeth gnashing against each other, her head jerking from side to side, whipping her red tresses from one shoulder to the other in a frantically building rhythm. In response he moved into longer, smoother strokes that brought his cock almost all the way out from her vaginal sheath, her little cunt-lips clinging to it desperately to keep it from withdrawing completely. He thrust forward into her smooth, uplifted buttocks, feeling the rippling vaginal fluid gurgle in response, feeling her vaginal lips nibbling frantically at the long, spear-like mass of his flesh. His fingers clawed at the tight skin of her ass-cheeks and dug in hard, searching for her tiny anal opening.

"Aaauugh!" she gasped in painful protest as his outstretched middle finger wormed into her soft, rubbery anus and pushed hard against it.

"Ooohh no, not there!" she groaned louder this time at the outrageous intrusion.

But the older man didn't slow down for a second. Feverishly, he worked his finger around and around inside the tightly heated rectal passage, stretching the rubbery orifice wider and wider as he ground and jerked into her. She felt a second finger making its way into her tortured rear passage, and deep, guttural whimpers streamed crazily from her throat as her teeth gnashed uncontrollably and her body squirmed and twisted in a dance of lewd desire. The groans of protest, however, quickly dissolved to whimpers of renewed pleasure as her body grew accustomed to the unnatural invasion.

The director grinned as he felt young

Jefferson Peterson's wife begin slowly churning her ass-cheeks back on his fingers as he insinuated them methodically around the warm, rubbery depths, sending chilling sensations of delight rippling through her body. She was doubly impaled now with his rock-hard cock lodged deep in her pussy and his fingers shoved hard into her anal channel. Moaning incoherently beneath him, she began to twist and squeal in savage abandon, desperately working herself toward orgasm.

* * *

Christ, that chick in the boardroom – whoever she was – had gone completely haywire, Jefferson Peterson mused as he watched the savage pantomime of their sex-play from his position on the balcony. He wondered who she was and whether he had seen her before in his few short weeks at work. The thought of another libertine like Jennifer getting a stiff cock rammed into her pussy stimulated him with wild runaway fantasies. Hell, he wouldn't mind having a tumble with her himself, but there was probably a waiting list if he judged his suspicions about the place correctly. It seemed that everybody around the place was on the make and that they were all getting it too. God, what a place to work! He'd never seen anything like it before.

"Ummh, look at them go," Jennifer purred, draping herself over his shoulder. "Old Stephen Marlingham can really swing it around, can't he?"

Even in the semi-darkness of the evening light Jefferson could see her eyes gleaming with reawakened arousal.

"Damn, I wish we could get closer somehow. I'd like to know who she is. She looks like she let out all the stops."

"We could try the windows; one of them must be open," she said impishly. "They'll be so busy they won't even know we're spying on them. Come on."

She grabbed his hand once again and guided him over to the windows at the far end of the balcony, giving them a careful push. He caught his breath as he saw them sliding open. Jennifer, on her tiptoes, squeezed into the crack into the boardroom.

Suddenly a piercing scream wracked the room, and for a moment Jefferson thought it was because the woman had spotted them surreptitiously entering... but no, he was safe, he realised a moment later. It was just that her wail signified that she was quickly approaching orgasm.

"Ooohhh, God, yes, fuck me harder!" she gasped obscenely.

Jefferson and Jennifer were behind a comfortable stuffed leather chair now, peering over the back-rest toward the centre of the room where the hot and heavy action was taking place. The young scientist sucked in his breath with surprise because never in his life had he seen such an exhibition of wanton sexuality and unadulterated lust. True, he'd just come like a bull into Jennifer Wilson's eager mouth only a few minutes ago, but even so he could feel his cock throbbing crazily at the sight of the two coupled bodies on the big, white sofa in the boardroom. From where they were hiding he couldn't see the couple's faces but had a good view of the lower portions of their bodies. He could see Marlingham's cock buried deep in the girl's pink cunt as she writhed savagely beneath him, twitching and spasming in the throes of uncontrolled lust.

Something struck him at that moment – a strange thought – and he moved out on his hands and knees from behind the chair where they'd been hiding. There was something vaguely familiar about the woman, but what was it? He couldn't put his finger on it immediately in his half-dazed state. But the closer he moved the more he was distracted by the physical action that was taking place, driving his mind away from the purpose of discovery. The girl was chanting hoarsely, as though possessed by some sort of sexual demon, her legs were drawn back as far as they could go and her hands were frenziedly clawing at the director's naked buttocks, digging deep into his flesh as she pulled him tighter and tighter against her loins.

Damn, she was one hot little bitch, he thought as he involuntarily began stroking his rock-hard cock through the confines of his pants. She was taking Marlingham's prick like she wanted it rammed all the way up to her throat.

"Damn, I want her next," he whispered out loud, barely conscious that he was talking to himself. Before he knew it, Jennifer had crawled up behind him and put her hands lightly on his shoulders.

"I hope they're giving you some ideas," she whispered. "I'm going crazy just watching them."

"You're going crazy. Jesus, what do you think is happening to me?"

"Old Marlingham really moves, doesn't he?"

"Goddamn, I'd heard rumours about him, but I never expected to see anything like this from one of the world's greatest scientists."

"Maybe he's just experimenting. Maybe he's going to write a scholarly paper on human reproductive systems," she giggled into his ear.

But Jefferson was hardly paying any attention to her, his eyes and ears focused on

the salacious fucking that was taking place only a few feet away. All fear of being discovered eavesdropping by the director had vanished now. After all, what was Marlingham going to do? Fire him when he had seen Marlingham having intercourse with a woman in the boardroom? No, he was perfectly safe and totally fascinated as well.

"Now, Stephen, now, please!" the naked woman begged. "Fuck harder, give it to me now… all the way in. Yess, yesss! Aaaggghhh! Like that!"

Suddenly the shock of recognition hit him like a fist in the stomach. That voice… he was sure of it… It was… it was his wife's voice. Marlingham was screwing his wife! Oh Jesus God, it was too incredible to be true.

The bewildered young husband's mind whirled in disbelief at the shadowy vision before his eyes. His first impulse was to run forward and rescue her from the lust-crazed director, but he knew this was no rape. He had seen how she was enjoying every second of being fucked by another man.

Paralysed, Jefferson stood, frozen as he heard her shrilly screaming out her orgasm, her legs splaying wide until he thought her cunt would split up the middle. Then he watched as Marlingham pushed her knees back cruelly over her shoulders, bending her double. God, no, she'd never be able to take it that deep, never. But in a moment, as he watched her body jerking and spasming to final fulfilment, he saw how wrong he'd been. Jesus, she was taking every thick, bludgeoning inch of it all right and moaning with pleasure even in her contorted position. Then she was screaming.

"Aaaaiiieee! I'm coming! I'm coming!"

The fucking bitch, he raged to himself. That little slut! She's loving it, she's moving her body like a bitch on heat. And all the time she's been giving me that babe-in-arms bit, trying to keep me a distance from her. And now – now this! Hate raging inside him, he watched the older man's buttocks twitch as his heated cum burst out of his ejaculating penis buried deep inside Catherine's cunt. When Marlingham finally withdrew himself from between her legs, Jefferson could stand it no longer.

"Damn you, get off her!" he raged, pushing Marlingham aside. "I oughta knock your teeth down your throat..." He caught himself mid-sentence, his voice cracking with emotion until he turned to Catherine.

"You slut," he roared. "You cheap, goddamn whore!"

"Oh no," Catherine groaned in humiliation at her husband seeing her naked and unprotected on the couch, her belly filled with another man's cum. She closed her eyes tight as though to blot out the sight of him standing over her, but she knew it was useless and that what was happening was real, not some sort of horrible nightmare. There was nothing she could do as his gaze travelled disdainfully over her naked and abused body. Marlingham, for his part, wasn't the least embarrassed as he picked himself up off the floor and grinned at his young employee with a lewd smile on his face. With a casual calm, he began dressing himself.

"Just keep cool, young fellow. I see you didn't barge in here alone."

"What the hell are you telling me to keep cool for after you just fucked my wife? I saw every second of it." Jefferson's fist was doubled up and his whole body was trembling.

In response Marlingham strode over to the chair in the far corner of the room and led Jennifer Wilson out to where they were all gathered.

"How was he?" he asked with a knowing look on his face. Jennifer responded only with a Mona Lisa-like smile.

How could Marlingham possibly know, Jefferson wondered. He was bluffing, just trying to get out of his own predicament.

As if reading his mind, Marlingham turned to him calmly.

"You're right, we saw everything. We saw

it from the staff lounge. You thought nobody would walk in on you in the lab, didn't you?"

"What are you talking about? I don't believe you."

"Come, come now, don't try to lie your way out of it. We saw just as much as you saw now, and so we decided to do the same thing. Fair play, isn't it?"

Jefferson stammered hopelessly, confused between anger and shame, but there was no way out. Marlingham obviously wasn't bluffing, but how had he happened to walk in at just the right moment? Suddenly he realised he'd been betrayed and he turned on Jennifer Wilson.

"You planned this, didn't you? The both of you."

"Very good," Marlingham laughed. "I was wondering how long it would take to dawn on you."

"Damn it," Jefferson hissed angrily. "Goddammit!"

Marlingham raised his eyebrows and chuckled, turning to Catherine who was slipping into her clothes, a despairing expression on her face.

"Well, I must say it worked out well. Even better than I expected. You have a hell of a wife, Peterson. I want you both to know you've been accepted into our little group here. You might call it extracurricular research studies. We do a little experimenting on our own after hours."

Both Catherine and Jefferson stared at him in utter amazement. Then Jefferson's eyes went back to his wife, focusing on the sticky strands of sperm that leaked out from her cunt as she hurriedly tried to slip her panties on.

His anger under control now, he began to speak in a low, sombre voice, dripping with sarcasm.

"That's just wonderful. I haven't been satisfied with what I've been getting at home. Maybe Catherine has learned some new things she can show me."

As these words rang in her ears, Catherine lifted her eyes to stare at the people gathered around her. She felt dazed and confused, overwhelmed by all the events that had happened so quickly. Her life was disrupted and broken in half, and what was happening now had an air of total unreality. She couldn't believe that both she and her husband had been so vilely tricked. She didn't know what to think except that everything she was hearing went against what she had been taught, everything she had believed in. It just wasn't right.

"No," she hissed vehemently. "I'm not

getting involved in anything like that. I won't have it. You're sick, all of you!"

"Sick, huh?" her husband snapped. "You're talking like some kind of innocent virgin again, and that sure as hell isn't the way you were acting a minute ago."

"Yes, and what happened to you?" Catherine sneered. "I suppose you were just doing research in the lab with that... that friend of yours. Just go ahead, you're free to do what you want, but you're not getting me involved in this kind of thing."

"All right, be quiet the both of you," the director growled authoritatively, cutting Jefferson off from replying. "If you want to continue here, you'll both cooperate. Otherwise there'll be a lot of trouble." His eyes narrowed ominously and he focused them on the husband and wife in turn. "If you try to get out of this there's going to be a lot of trouble for everyone. You remember a certain packet of photos in the desk, don't you, Catherine? I hope you realise your fingerprints are all over them, and it might be embarrassing if word of that leaked out. So you can see we're all in this together."

The young wife's eyes narrowed as she gazed at Marlingham, trembling with hostility. So, he had planted the envelopes too. It was all a trick. She'd been trapped, she and

Jefferson too, though that didn't make things any easier to take.

"You wouldn't dare do a thing like that," she spat.

"Oh yes, I would, and I've done other things just like it. Our little group here has been going on for a long time and we've managed to preserve the utmost secrecy." She watched as he smiled confidently, enunciating his words with calm composure. "We've had to be pretty clever to preserve the anonymity of our group, and we've succeeded. So, don't try going against the tradition. You'll both be cut down quicker than you think. I'm sure you understand."

"Photographs? What the hell are you talking about?" Jefferson asked, a puzzled frown contorting his face. It seemed like the whole trap had been set much more carefully than he had figured.

"Just relax," Marlingham soothed. "Your wife can give you the details later. I'm in a bit of a hurry now but, before I go, let me tell you the first meeting will be tomorrow night at my place. Plan on being there, because if you aren't..."

He needn't have bothered completing the sentence, for both Catherine and Jefferson Peterson knew exactly what he meant, and what was more, they knew that he would follow through on his threats.

Jennifer had been sitting down listening to the conversation with an impassive expression on her face. She was casually smoking a cigarette and tilting her head back as she blew jets of air toward the ceiling.

"I think they understand now," she said coldly to the director. "I'd appreciate it if you'd give me a ride home. I'm in just as much of a hurry as you are."

"All right, I think I've gotten my message across. I'll expect to see both of you at my place at nine o'clock. Be there."

Perfectly in command, Marlingham escorted Jennifer from the room, leaving the distraught husband and wife facing each other. The tension grew quietly between them until finally Catherine broke from the strain. With her blouse half-unbuttoned she rushed over to Jefferson and threw her arms around him.

"Oh God, honey, forgive me. I'm so sorry," she begged, sobs choking her throat. "They tricked us. They tricked both of us. What are we going to do about that meeting tomorrow? I'm so afraid."

Stonily, the young scientist backed away from his pleading wife, a frown of distaste disfiguring his forehead. "We're going, that's what we're doing," he said. "And don't think everything's going to be all right. I saw what you did, and I'm not going to forgive you for a long, long time."

Suddenly a flush of anger flooded Catherine's cheeks.

"How can you say that? How can you possibly be so hypocritical? Have you forgotten that I witnessed everything you did? Everything." How dare he treat me like this, she thought bitterly. After all he's done he actually has the nerve to act so damn self-righteous and unforgiving. Does he think I'm the only one to blame?

In a day that had already wracked her nerves this was the last straw. Her eyes blazing, she wordlessly gripped her handbag and headed for the door, turning off the light on her way out. Let him find his own way, she said bitterly to herself. If he wanted to play dirty, so could she. One thing was sure. Their life together was going to change very quickly. He was going to pay for the way he'd humiliated her, and she was going to make sure that the price was big.

Chapter 8

Catherine couldn't help feeling nervous as Stephen Marlingham led them through his home the following evening. It was located only five miles or so from the centre in a secluded pine area, and it had the aura of a Southern mansion of the type she'd only seen in movies before. Tall, stately pillars graced the front; colonial windows with freshly painted shutters broke up the whiteness of the façade, but the exterior was only an introduction to the magnificence of the inside.

The furniture was richly varnished colonial, and the walls were decorated with prints of horses and hunting scenes. Expensive-looking art objects perched on every table, and the carpeting was so plush that she nearly sank into it with each step.

"Where is everyone? I thought this was supposed to be some kind of a meeting?"

"Just relax," the director chuckled casually. "Everyone is downstairs in the games room. Appropriate name for the place, don't you think? I just had it soundproofed. There aren't many neighbours around here, but things get noisy at times, you know."

Her whole body trembled nervously as the older scientist's remarks reminded her of their purpose at his home tonight. Good God, how would she ever get through the evening? Desperately, she wished Jefferson could offer her some kind of support, but since yesterday he'd hardly spoken to her or even looked at her, for that matter.

In truth, up until this moment, she hadn't worried about his behaviour, confident that eventually they would make peace and things would be all right. In a way, too, she'd been looking forward to this evening to avenge herself for the way he'd reacted to discovering her and Marlingham. In the final analysis it had been his fault to begin with, and though he had chastised her, it was really she who wouldn't be able to forgive him for a long, long time.

The events of the previous afternoon had changed things so that they would never be the same again. And it wasn't just that she had discovered him in the naked embrace of another woman. No, the change was deeper than that and reflected something that was going on inside herself, for she'd come to the conclusion that she'd enjoyed having sex with Stephen Marlingham. It had been a great shock, of course, but had liberated a long-smouldering desire that had lain dormant inside her for God knew how long. It was so ironic that though her husband had tried to do the same thing, it was a total stranger who had finally succeeded – a stranger who'd come into her life to set her wild and free. For the first time she knew that sex didn't necessarily have to be bound up with love, but was a rich and rewarding experience in itself. She'd learned that she could make her own body give her pleasure if only she could loosen up and be prepared for that pleasure. It was simply a question of attitude, and Stephen Marlingham had changed her attitude in a shockingly short time.

The worst of it all was that she wasn't totally certain that she could ever be satisfied with one man again. For if she had felt more fulfilment than ever under the ministrations of a perfect stranger, what was to stop that experience from repeating itself ad infinitum? Tonight would be the test, and she was praying that somehow she would fail, that she would just be a normal housewife again – an everyday woman who could remain content with the man she happened to be married to.

Pondering these thoughts, Catherine walked demurely between the director and her husband down the staircase to the basement level, where the games room was located. Though dimly lit, the room was filled with party noises, indicating a large crowd. Some couples were dancing, some talking loudly and others were spread out on the long, low, leather couches that lined the walls. All this was normal for any party, but what left her in shocked surprise was that not a soul was wearing a stitch of clothing. Her knees and hands trembled as she beheld the sight, for now she knew that the real test of her new resolve had arrived.

Flabby, skinny, young and middle-aged,

everyone casually occupied himself as though he were at a normal cocktail party in a suburban household, as though it would be ludicrous for them to cover themselves. The three of them, not the others, were the ones who looked ridiculous now, they were so out of place with their clothes on. Jefferson, she guessed, who was standing behind her, was undoubtedly thinking the same thing.

A moment later, Marlingham had separated from them and gone over to a strange, large object in one corner of the room, which, through the darkness, she hadn't noticed before. It was situated by a door that led out from the games room and was large and cubical in size, covered by a heavy, velvet curtain with a metal ladder hooked to one side. What in the world was it, she wondered. It looked like a giant box of some sort, but why the curtains, what were they supposed to hide?

Her concentration was interrupted, however, by the director clapping his hands sharply and demanding everyone's attention.

"Please... everyone... I have an announcement to make. We have a new couple tonight. A new addition to our group." His eyes twinkled gaily as his voice carried over the attentive listeners in the room. "I know both these people will be a great asset to our activities tonight and many nights to come. Now if you'll help to take their clothes off, we'll begin our initiation ceremonies."

As he paused for a moment, Catherine suddenly realised that she was the centre of attention, the focus of the hungry glances of the males surrounding her. She wouldn't be safe, she realised, even if she had worn a suit of armour. She felt naked now, having been undressed by their ravenous gazes, and instinctively her hand went up to break the low décolletage of her dress.

Smiling benignly, the director continued, "As you can see, the young lady is a little shyer than her husband. But shyness is becoming in our females, isn't it? Ladies and gentlemen, let's give our new members a big, hearty welcome."

The scene was so absurd she could hardly believe it. Marlingham had introduced them as though they were performers about to enter on a stage, but instead of applause, they were greeted by a stammering silence and the crude looks that bespoke naked sexuality, unadorned by any pretence of manners.

"Well, start mingling, people," Marlingham urged. "And as for you two, start taking your clothes off. What do you think this is – a formal ball?"

As the director finished speaking, Catherine was aware of the glances turned on her, and the fear which had seized her earlier turned to blind panic. She whirled around, whispering urgently to her husband.

"Jefferson, please, we've got to get out of here."

The words caught in her throat and she was just about to break up into sobs as she saw her husband begin to unbutton his shirt, all the while staring at her with a contemptuous look on his face.

"What's the matter?" he sneered. "Too many men for you? I'm sure you can handle them all after the way I saw you working out with Marlingham." Suddenly, he brushed by her and headed into the crowd, stripping his shirt off as he did so. Tears of despair choked in her eyes, but with an effort, she managed to control herself. Damn him, she raged inwardly. If this is what he wants, he'll get it all right. She wasn't going to back out now. She was going to follow it all the way through to the bitter end. The names he had called her – 'whore', 'slut' – rang in her ears, but she told herself that he was really going to find out what they meant tonight. She was going to give him a dose of medicine so powerful she hoped he would choke on it.

Mustering her courage, she turned to face the naked men who had slowly closed in on her. She didn't recognise them from the Centre or anywhere else, and they seemed like crude, vulgar types who were eyeing her as though she were a meal to be enjoyed.

"Hiya, Catherine," the tall one in the middle said. "My name's Sam Landers. I'm the Mayor of Fort Bridge." She tried to contain herself and smile at him, but noticing the lecherous glint in his eye, a chill of anxiety shot up her spine.

"H-hello," she stammered nervously, unable to figure out what to say next. She couldn't very well talk about her job or politics at a time like this. She relaxed a little when Landers began speaking in a smooth, charming voice.

"Why don't ya'll just let your hair down? After all, everybody's friends here."

God, she thought, it was just like a regular cocktail party except that everyone else was naked and she wasn't. Her nerves subsiding, she found herself able to speak a little more easily.

"Thank you... I mean, I really don't know what to say. I've never seen anything like this before."

"Don't worry, Catherine. You'll get used to it. It's not as bad as you think."

"Come on, Mayor, stop pussy-footin' around. Let's get on with this. I want a bit of her before we leave tonight."

The gruff voice suddenly shattered Catherine's composure, and she stared nervously at the stubby, broad-chested man who had just interrupted the Mayor. Her eyes fastened involuntarily on the long, thick rod of his penis that was hanging like a bullwhip between his legs, looking as though it were ready to spring into action at any second.

"You like that, doncha, baby?" he guffawed, catching the look in her eyes. "Well, you're gonna see plenty of it tonight, and you can tell that fancy-pants husband of yours that you got it from Steve Haskins. I'm the police chief in case you're interested. And I got more cock than anybody else in this room. You're gonna be calling me up on the phone asking for more after you see the way I give it to ya tonight."

Catherine shuddered in repulsion, wondering how she could ever let a horrible-looking man like him touch her. She looked at the other two in the group, hoping that somehow she would be spared the stubby little police chief, but she saw no trace of compassion in their eyes. The Mayor, however, resumed his conversation as though the chief's remarks had been just an annoying interjection.

"This is John Furrow, head of Furrow Construction company, and this is John's son, James. He's captain of the football team at Fort Bridge High School."

Catherine's heart fluttered as she gazed at

the boy. He was built like a Greek god, with rippling stomach muscles and sinewy forearms and biceps. His cock was youthful-looking, but large for his age, and Catherine, though she tried to avert her eyes, found herself looking at it. The expression on the boy's face was that of a naïve teenager, lacking the sophistication of his mature body. She wondered how long he'd been a part of this group that Marlingham had assembled. She wondered even more how Marlingham had gathered these people all together under one roof in the first place. Originally she thought it would be people from work, but now it seemed as though the whole town of Fort Bridge had come to the director's mansion to participate in the orgy or whatever they called it.

Looking from face to face in the group assembled around her, she saw no compassion in anyone's eyes, no pity for her plight. How could she possibly go through with this? How could she possibly allow herself to be fucked by all these men? She had to stall them, that was it. She had to make mindless conversation until she found a means to slip away.

"Tell me, how did you all get to know Dr Marlingham?" she asked as pleasantly as she could.

In unison the men guffawed amongst each other until they'd finally recovered enough for the Mayor to speak.

"We didn't get to know Dr Marlingham. Dr Marlingham got to know us. He's the one that started all this, and you know in a small town like Fort Bridge it's hard to keep any secrets. When Steve here found out about the orgies going on, we took the matter up with Stephen Marlingham himself."

"Y-you mean, you knew there were things like this going on and you didn't do anything about it?"

"Hell," the police chief growled, "we did somethin' all right. We joined the club, and now practically the whole town's here tonight."

Her small talk was not going the way she expected, for any minute she feared they were going to drag her off some place. If only she could find Jefferson and plead with him to help her. She would even beg his forgiveness just to get out of here. But no, she knew he wouldn't do anything like that. He was still too bitter and wanted to hurt her.

The police chief, who was swishing his drink around in his hand, looked up at her again.

"Ain't you ever wondered what that thing is?" he said, pointing toward the large, cubical object covered with heavy curtains.

"I... I was looking at it when we came in."

"Well, come on, I'll show ya," he said,

rudely grasping her by the arm. "You ain't gonna believe this."

Catherine could feel her heart pounding in her throat, as the short, barrel-chested man was about to lead her off.

"No, please... I'm not really that curious. Not now. I think maybe I'd better just go."

"Go? Hell, you can't go yet. You gotta take a good look-see at this here contraption that Stephen Marlingham dragged into this house. You ain't never gonna see anything like it again."

The man had gripped her elbow and was tugging it insistently now, and she knew she had no choice but to follow him where he was taking her or create an unpleasant scene. Desperately, her eyes searched the room for her husband until finally she sighted him over by one of the couches being administered to by three naked women.

Catherine balked for a minute, her gaze lingering. All the girls were concentrating on arousing Jefferson and themselves as well. Two of them were taking turns licking and sucking his cock, while the third was down on her knees between his legs eagerly massaging his balls with a soft squeezing action. Catherine's stomach was about to turn in disgust when the police chief gave her a final no-nonsense tug on the arm and led her toward the door next to the veiled object.

"Let's stop messin' around here, woman. I got somethin' to show you," he said impatiently.

In a kind of hypnotic trance she allowed herself to enter through the doorway, growing angrier and angrier by the second as she thought about how well her husband was adapting to the situation. Imagine the nerve he had to call her terrible things – things like 'whore' and 'slut' – as though she were the one who was supposed to be moral while he was free to do anything he wanted. She was sick of his double standards and determined to punish him, and with all her heart she hoped somehow Jefferson could see her when she was being fucked by these men. Resigning herself to her fate she found herself walking along a dark, carpeted corridor accompanied by the four men. It looked almost like some sort of secret passageway fitting for an old Southern mansion, but in a matter of moments she realised it was leading them back to more or less where they'd come from.

"Why are we going away from the others?"

"Hell, woman," the police chief laughed. "I told you we were going to show you this thing here, and that's what I'm doing now."

Flicking on a light switch, he opened the door and moved forward until Catherine found herself in a kind of glass enclosed box, open at the top and covered with sand and rocks on the bottom. She realised she was inside the curtain-covered cube she had seen earlier.

"What is this? Where are we?"

"We're in an aquarium, for God's sake. Don't you know an aquarium when you see one? Same thing as they got in them labs at Ellsworth-Cima Research. Only this one ain't gonna get you wet, so you don't have to worry about that pretty little body of yours."

Catherine could hardly believe that Marlingham was so perverted as to actually transport an aquarium into his own home as a setting for the orgiastic lovemaking that went on there.

"Sort of love in a goldfish bowl," the Mayor laughed as he stepped inside behind her, followed by the other two.

"But what about the curtains? Nobody will be able to see us in here," Catherine protested. If she were to go through with this at all, it would be so that her husband would witness it. He had to! She desperately wanted to punish him.

"Hell, don't you worry your sweet little ass about that," the police chief soothed her. "When we start really goin' at it, one of us'll pull the string here, and then everybody in the room can see what's goin' on. It'll be just like a stag movie, only better."

The men and the teenage boy looked at each other, unable to conceal the grins of lustful excitement that spread across their faces. She just hoped she could let herself go tonight and not suddenly get cold feet and back out. Most of all, she hoped her husband would see her inside the tank when the curtains suddenly drew apart.

She wondered now whether she might not have let the men think she was too willing. After all, they might make her do what she'd seen the woman in the lab doing to her husband. But if she had to suck their cocks, she would just have to live through the experience somehow, guided by the need to shock her husband like he'd never been shocked before.

"What do you say we all get started with the evening's entertainment?" the police chief suggested, and as if to obey his command, pairs of hands reached out and began undressing her. She felt her zipper swishing down, her straps being slid off her shoulders; and then someone behind her was down on his knees slowly gliding the hem of her slip upward and removing it over her shoulders. Another pair of hands jerked at her brassiere and unsnapped it while at the same time she found her panties being rolled down over her hips and buttocks.

She could hardly believe she was letting

this happen to her, but there was no way to deny that it was really taking place. She was standing naked in a giant fish bowl about to be ravished by four men. How in the world could it be true? And how could she not be resisting them?

The truth was that, far from resisting, she felt nervous only from a sense of excitement at the impending adventure. She was actually looking forward to what was going to happen to her.

"Man, get a look at that ass," the police chief sighed appreciatively from behind her. In spite of her mesmerised state, Catherine could feel herself blushing from the remark, and she turned to look at the others who were appraising and evaluating her as though she were merchandise on a slave market.

"Well, gentlemen, I think she's about ready for her initiation," the Mayor announced as she stood perfectly still. Her mind was somewhere far away, but her ears were tuned to the sounds coming from the room on the other side of the curtain. She could hear gasps and moans building in rhythmic progression and an occasional shriek as one of the women reached the point of orgasm.

She came quickly back to reality as she saw the four men begin to close in on her in a tight circle, sending a momentary shiver of fear up her spine. She jumped as though touched by a live wire when one of the men suddenly reached out and stroked her buttocks.

"Just relax now," the Mayor said. "You were doing fine a minute ago."

"Maybe she'd like it in that tight little ass of hers," Haskins, the police chief, grinned. His bulky little body moved closer, and she could feel his finger worming its way into the crevice between her buttocks, making her squirm slightly. "Damn, you got some little ass. I'd like to split it in half with this cock of mine!"

God, what had she gotten herself into now? Her head downcast, she sensed the teenage boy approaching and watched as he slowly bent down on his knees with an excited expression on his face and used his thumb and forefinger to part the soft, curling strands of her pubic hair.

"Oh wow, what a pussy!" he exclaimed. "Man, I'm gonna get some of that to eat before we fuck her!"

"That sounds like a good idea," the Mayor agreed. "However, as the highest ranking official present, I believe the first honours should go to me. It's about time we started the show rolling anyway."

Grasping her hand, he led her out from the circle formed by the others and guided her down onto the smooth, white sand

that lined the bottom of the tank. The three other men followed them over while the Mayor lay down next to her. They watched, their lust-twisted faces contorted into masks of naked desire. It was like some kind of tribal rite, but there was nothing she could do about it. She had gotten herself into this and now she would have to follow it through, no matter what happened, no matter what they did to her. She was alone and completely at their mercy. Suddenly she felt gruff hands pinning down her shoulders and saw Steve Haskins standing in between her legs, his cock erect and rigid, hovering menacingly above her, his balls dangling beneath it like bloated, water-filled balloons.

For a moment she thought she might pass out, even prayed for it to happen, but suddenly the Mayor rose to his feet and took command of the situation.

"Wait a minute, Steve," he said sternly. "I thought we had the priorities straightened out here. Besides, if you go first, there isn't going to be anything left of her. I think she needs a little loosening up anyway."

"Okay," the police chief grumbled, stepping back. "But you better not screw it up."

The others were gathered in a semicircle now as the Mayor sank down to his knees between her legs and pressed his lips against her naked belly.

"Go on, lick it, Mayor. Suck that cunt!" she could hear the chief's voice urging him on.

Convulsively her stomach spasmed as Landers began to glide his wetly glistening lips over her flesh. She tried to cringe away from the sudden contact, but it was impossible, and an involuntary chill raced up the length of her spine. Then she felt the Mayor's tongue tracing downward to her crotch, his tongue moving like a quivering snake into the tight, moist slit of her pussy.

Automatically her body responded with convulsive jerks and twitches, a loud, shattering moan pouring from her lips. She felt him rudely clamp his sweating palms against the trembling insides of her cream-white thighs, spreading them wider to have greater access to her loins. She forced her head up off the sand, her eyes wide and terror-stricken as she saw him hunched like an animal on all fours, grinning up at her like a coiled beast about to pounce on its prey. The pinkly glistening flesh of her moist vagina was presented up to his leering face like a pagan sacrifice.

A groan came from the Mayor's throat as he harshly sucked in his breath and unpeeled the ragged pink lips of her vagina with his thumbs. His eyes fixed on the sight, and suddenly with a greedy hunger, he dipped his head down, and with a maddening sucking noise, drew the tiny pink bud of Catherine's throbbing clitoris into his hungrily gaping mouth. He nibbled at it with the edges of his teeth, feeling it spring to life.

Catherine clenched her eyes tight against the swirling spirals of strange sensations that were rocketing through her pinioned body. She fought with all her strength against the lewd sensations that were building inside her, but in spite of her repulsion at being forced into such a degrading and humiliating situation, trembling sparks of raw pleasure were beginning to ignite her dormant womb.

With a sudden jerk, the Mayor's tongue slipped forward, burrowing deep into her tightly clasped cunt like a racing lizard, and she realised it was no longer possible to deny the latent sensations within that begged to be released. She recalled her earlier resolve of going along with everything these men demanded of her and suddenly realised that her intense psychological preparations had been unnecessary. For now she was sure they could force her to do any perverted thing they desired and she would be unable to resist. She had no choice but to admit that she was actually enjoying what was happening to her now. True, flashes of regret were beginning to trouble her, but then she remembered how her husband had obviously been enjoying the attention of all those women on the couch in the other room. Why shouldn't she have the same opportunity? She was sick and tired of his chauvinistic double standards, and now she was determined to liberate herself completely from all the puritanical bonds of the past that had tied her down.

The image of her husband being sucked and licked by the strange women around him danced through her mind as she surrendered to the shocks of pleasure rippling through her body while the Mayor's quick-moving tongue speared in and out of her dilated vagina. Suddenly, her reason deserted her as her body responded more and more feverishly to the oral manipulations of her frantically quivering cunt. Her hips jerked up spasmodically, burying the flicking tongue to its roots.

Never before had she experienced such wanton abandon, and for the first time she cared about nothing else. Not her husband, her principles, nor the humiliations she was undergoing. All that mattered was the hotly flicking tongue diving in and out of her cunt, mining her for the rich liquid of her loins. Her buttocks ground and grated against the sand beneath her, as though trying to extinguish the hot fire of her loins, trying to subdue the flicking tongue that lashed into her pussy.

She'd never realised before what it meant to be a truly sensual woman, free to work out the accumulated frustrations of years she had devoted to protecting her reputation and innocence, free from months of fighting off her husband's 'improper' advances.

But why were her inhibitions so suddenly released? Perhaps it was the fact that these men were strangers, or that she was almost completely at their mercy. She didn't know for sure, but her inner fears had dissipated, and she was now willing to give them whatever they wanted. Something had turned her body on, and she prayed for her and Jefferson's sake that it wouldn't soon be turned off.

Straining against the arms that restrained her, she thrust her pelvis upward, feverishly grinding her cunt against the Mayor's face buried in between her legs. She began churning her buttocks in tight teasing circles, fighting for the release that was now so close. Suddenly the Mayor thrust his head back, withdrawing his tongue from her cunt, raising himself up as he pushed against her thighs.

"Not now... don't stop now," she wailed, as she saw him backing away and slowly rising to his feet. "P-p-p-please, suck me. Oh God, suck my cunt. Don't go away!"

Her eyes frosted with desire, she searched the men looming about her until finally the police chief grinned down at her and, gripping her hand, hoisted her up to a sitting position. She needed one thing now, and one thing only – a cock! God, she would do anything for a cock between her legs.

"Hurry! Please. Fast!" she begged as the short, stubby man insinuated himself between her legs. He draped her legs over his thighs and waddled closer as she grasped his cock and tightly circled her fingers around it. It was thick and filled with blood, and she guided it hungrily in between her gaping cunt-lips.

Suddenly, like a live, wet animal she could feel it sliding into her, his balls smacking heavily on her upturned ass, his hairy stomach grating against the yielding softness of her belly.

She strained against him, silently pleading for him to go deeper into her belly.

"Deeper, deeper. Fuck me deeper!" she wailed, squirming and jerking like a trapped animal.

Clutching the cheeks of her ass he pitched his hips forward, sinking his cock inside her cunt up to the hilt.

Groaning in frustration, she knew that she needed more, that he wasn't big enough for her. She splayed her legs wider, her knees pointing upward to give him greater access, but it was hardly worth it. His jerking cock pistoned into her with rampant excitement, but it still didn't go deep enough to please her. Her whole body strained, gasps and moans escaping from her lips as his pelvis smacked against her loins, a brutal thud resounding with each thrust. She moaned again, this time like a cat on heat as he strained to bring her to climax with the brutal pounding of his body. She bucked beneath him, concentrating with all her might on the elusive apex of orgasm, and suddenly she felt his cock flesh stiffen and jerk, spewing its stored-up juices far up inside the secret recesses of her gaping womb.

But it wasn't enough. Oh God, why couldn't he satisfy her? She felt the keen frustration of disappointment as tears ran down her reddened cheeks. Before she knew it, though, the police chief had fallen back to be replaced by the contractor, a burly, grey-haired man with a powerful, well-preserved, middle-aged body.

Lifting her head up slightly she gazed down in between her widespread legs to observe his cock as he knelt before her. It was huge and thick, lined with powerful blue veins, and it jutted out from between his legs like a threatening spear, his testicles dangling beneath it like powerful balled fists. She knew it would be like a telephone pole ramming inside her, but all resistance and sense of morality had deserted her, and she was ready for it now.

"Yes, give it to me," she hissed through clenched teeth. "Ram it inside my pussy."

"Damn right I will, baby. Damn right," he said, grinning, his lips bared back over his teeth. Gripping his hand around the inflamed organ he began to stroke it back and forth as she watched it growing in length and breadth before her very eyes. God, how much bigger could it get? She could never take it as it was now, but she needed it, she needed it with all her heart!

"Come on, hurry," she rasped throatily. "Stick it in me, quick!"

The other men were on their knees around her in a tight vicious circle, their faces leering down at her, evil grins of malicious lust on their lips. They were practically panting as they watched the contractor preparing himself to fuck her. Quickly they swung into action, strong hands grasping her ankles and stretching her legs flat and wide apart, other hands pressing her shoulders down flat in the sand. Her hair-covered pussy was stretched wide apart, the tiny lips gaping eagerly as though desperately desiring to be fed with a thick, bulging staff of male flesh. Slowly the contractor guided his cock forward until the quivering, blood-filled head found the opening of her cunt and then it rested there for a long tantalising moment.

"Go on, ram it in her, daddy," the teenage

boy urged excitedly, watching his father manoeuvre his cock into position. His eyes were bulging and he had grasped his youthful cock with one hand, rubbing the foreskin slowly back and forth.

His father was grinning insanely, his face contorted with a raw lust such as she'd never seen before. Suddenly he flicked his hips forward and the bloated cockhead insinuated itself in between her cunt-lips so that they reacted with an automatic spasm, clenching tightly around the instrument. Another quick lurch and he was in deeper, bringing another worldly moan from Catherine's throat as she gritted her teeth sharply together.

"Just you sit tight, baby. This ain't even started yet," she could hear a gruff voice warning her. "Shit, you got two more to go and then some. You're gonna have plenty of cock tonight, sweetheart."

"Aaaugh!" she moaned again as the cock sank an inch deeper inside her. Her legs kicked and her body squirmed but she was held rigidly in place by pairs of stocky hands and arms, and she knew there was no escape. She had no choice but to enjoy every second of the tortured splitting of her lust-swollen cunt. She was certain her cunt-lips were going to be torn apart, her belly ripped asunder. The pain was unbearable, wracking her body like blows from bolts of lightning.

The grey-haired contractor levered up onto his knees, then came down hard on her with a thud, his grin widening as his cock seared deep up inside her pussy flesh.

"Awww!" she gasped, her head thrashing from side to side.

The rock-hard male cock sank in another inch, another excruciating inch into the tight, wet chamber of her abused vagina.

"Ummmppphhh! Awwwgh!" she groaned, her head twisting crazily from shoulder to shoulder.

Hot breath raked her naked, sweating body as the men crowded closer, hypnotised by the brutal skewering of her loins. Through the dimness of her confusion she was aware of hands clutching and squeezing her breasts, clawing over every part of her flesh until she felt as though she were being attacked by predatory animals trying to suck and scrape her flesh away from her bones.

She breathed and hissed frantically, her body bucking and jerking in a savage frenzy. Her sobbing struggles only seemed to excite her ravishers even more, and they clawed at her with abandoned ferocity. The body of the heavy man above her crashed down once again, his cock ploughing mindlessly into her cunt passage, pressing great waves of her pink flesh before it, smashing even the last mite of resistance in her soul. It was an uncontrolled demon crawling around inside her, filling her every crevice and knotting her inner organs in tight fists that could not breathe or move. She thought the jerking, pulsing rod would burst into her throat any minute if he didn't stop, so great was the pressure. It was ripping her soul from her body and devouring it in great gulps of depraved sensuality.

Suddenly it began to jerk and twist with a life of its own, entirely separate from the contractor's quickly working body. With an enormous thud, his sperm-bloated balls slapped against her ass-cheeks as he groaned above her like a wounded animal. The head flexed inside her and she groaned uncontrollably.

"Come, come, damn it!" she begged him, her eyes wide with urging.

In response he began sliding in and out with long, smooth strokes, and her groans became progressively quieter as she grew accustomed to the monstrous intrusion inside her. Then he began a slow revolving motion with his pelvis, grinding his bludgeon-like organ into her naked loins, expanding the tight-stretched interior of her vagina until it fitted him like a well-tailored glove.

The men around her stared wide-eyed, unbelieving that the tight, tiny cunt they had seen before could swallow the whole of the enormous cock buried inside it. From either side, in between her legs fingers teased at her hair-covered cunt-lips clinging tenaciously to the lust-bloated organ. She felt a finger from somewhere probing at her tightly clenched asshole, worming its way slowly into the velvety nether flesh. It curled like a corkscrew, slowly enlarging the tiny opening until the palm of the invading hand lay spread against her ass-cheeks, the finger sunk deep inside.

The contractor quickened his tempo now with an agonising bucking and jerking motion, ramming his cock quickly in and out of her hot, begging pussy. Her body and asscheeks ground helplessly into the sand as her legs kicked and jerked against the hands restraining her ankles. The finger buried deep in her asshole began to piston savagely in and out, matching the rhythm of the driving cock above it. Tortured grunts and groans poured from her throat as sweat coated her forehead.

The pain was miraculously diminishing and strange sensations of tingling excitement flooded her body to her very extremities. The outrageous humiliation and debasement she was undergoing aroused masochistic delights inside her which she could no longer deny. Her hips began gyrating in an abandoned tempo, matching the increased speed of the cock and finger fucking into her. Hands from all around her groped to drive her on as leering faces peered down hungrily.

"Aw! Agh! F-fuck me!" she crooned, her eyes darting about like those of a frantic animal. Hardened cocks were everywhere, quivering above her and pointing, poised at all parts of her body. No longer compelled to hold her down, the men had begun stroking them in time to the bucking of the jerking woman's hips. She was surrounded by them, imprisoned by them and all the time the most magnificent of them was fucking into her, expanding the walls of her loins with each savage stroke. For a moment she remembered that the curtain hadn't yet been opened and that her husband hadn't been able to see the degradation she was undergoing. She had almost forgotten the main reason why she'd allowed herself to do this. But there was nothing she could do, not now at this moment. She was a helpless captive against the lewd ravishment being inflicted on her by the four men.

"God, don't stop, please don't stop!" she gasped quickly, her brain reeling and whirling as she rotated her upthrust ass faster and faster in lewd, lascivious circles to keep pace with the monstrous cock flesh that was ramming ceaselessly into her. She could feel someone seizing her hand and placing his cock in it, and then her fingers automatically clasping around it and beginning to rub it back and forth in a maddening, sensual rhythm. No longer caring what was happening, she stroked it faster and faster, feeling it bulging and jerking in her hand.

Suddenly it jumped and as her eyes widened she could see quick jets of sperm leaping from its quivering head, raining down on her breasts like hail on a tarpaulin. At the same time, the contractor rolled his eyes and groaned, and suddenly his cock shot off like a firecracker, his bloated balls forcing gush after gush of white-hot cum deep into her loins. She ground her naked crotch up tight against his pelvis, her nibbling cunt-lips milking his penis clean until with a groan he fell back, his deflated cock popping out limply from her warm, sated pussy.

Under his giant body, Catherine sobbed with frustration. It just wasn't fair that she should be deprived of the climax she had fought for while these men used her body to satisfy their own selfish desires. Especially when Jefferson was having the time of his life on the other side of this strange aquarium, free to do what he wanted with all those women who'd clustered around him. It was the double standard again, and she thought she would never be able to conquer it. Then suddenly she remembered once again the whole purpose of why she was doing what she was doing. Opening her eyes, she shrieked a command at the lust-crazed men around her.

"Open the curtains, dammit. Now!"

To her surprise she could see the Mayor immediately jumping to her order and pulling the drawstrings so that the thick velvet curtain slid wide apart, revealing a view into the other room.

"Don't you worry about showing your husband," he chuckled. "We're not finished yet. No sir, not by any means."

"You bet your sweet little ass," Haskins, the police chief, guffawed.

"We got plenty more lead in our pencils."

"W-what are you going to do next?" Catherine demanded, her legs still splayed and thick streams of cum seeping out from her cunt and down the insides of her thighs.

"You'll see," the Mayor said. "Now get down on your hands and knees."

"Yeah, just like a bitch sheep dog," Haskins grinned lewdly.

Puzzled, she obeyed nevertheless, planting her knees in the gritty sand and supporting herself with her arms out in front of her. She suddenly felt the weight of the Mayor behind her, his hands stretching wide the white cheeks of her buttocks. Immediately she assumed that he was going to take advantage of her the way her husband had done last week and was comforted by the fact that not much more damage could be done to her vagina now after what she'd been through. It had horrified her then, but now she didn't care at all.

"Now just you relax," the Mayor comforted her. "You just take it nice and easy, even though it might be a little uncomfortable at first."

Slowly, two of his fingers wiggled into her asshole and began squirming around inside, widening the tight little ring until she could feel a cool breeze rushing inside. She found herself squirming her buttocks back against his ministrations, her sphincter muscles clasping and unclasping in a rhythmic cadence. Tiny moans of pleasure rippled from her lips as his feverish manipulations increased in intensity, bringing to her sensations she had never experienced before. Her willpower seemed to be entirely drained as her excitement built, and she felt herself desperately desiring that he would ram his stiff, male member inside as her husband had once done from that position.

"Come on, spread your legs, sweetheart," he demanded.

And automatically she could feel her knees sliding slowly apart on the gritty sand, expanding her anal passage wider and wider so that it could be abused by the man behind her. His finger continued to prod at the deep little hole as she winced, jumping forward slightly from the tense contact.

It entered slowly, not hurting as she'd anticipated but sending a sensation of surprised pleasure through her body as the finger wormed its way deeper and deeper into her rectum. With a sawing motion he began to draw it in and out, widening the tiny anus more and more. She cried out and grabbed the sand as though she were grasping for a branch to keep from falling off a cliff. He forced in another finger and this time it hurt. She winced with pain and tried to squirm away from the impalement, but the Mayor locked her close to him with one hand tightly clasped on her hip. For a brief moment he was still, then his fingers began working together inside her once again, corkscrewing into her asshole without mercy, stretching the tiny, puckered hole until she grunted in pain each time he twisted his hand.

The other men watched in fascination at the cruel subjugation of this lovely, young wife by the city official. Their jaws gaped with disbelief when suddenly Catherine's flushed face began to show joy. Her mouth hung open and she began panting and mewling as the Mayor's long fingers probed the depths of her asshole, and she rotated her buttocks back against his hand.

"Goddamn, jam that hand up in there!"

"Go to it, Mayor. Cornhole that sweet little bitch!"

"Waaa-hooo, can she move that ass!"

The excited noises grew loud and boisterous as though they were all at some kind of barn dance, and they whooped and hollered mercilessly as she began to respond to the skewering of her ass with abandoned fervour.

Suddenly she realised what the Mayor was preparing her for. He was going to stick his cock in her rectum! No, he couldn't possibly have meant it, she thought, as her mind raced like a forest fire out of control. That was a perversion so disgusting she could hardly imagine it. All the time she'd thought the Mayor was just priming her with foreplay to enter her vagina from the rear, and she had to admit how much it had stimulated her. In fact, she was so aroused she could barely stand it any longer! She wanted his cock, that big, bulging cock, sliding into her pussy flesh, not back there.

"Not my asshole!" she screamed back at him. "Don't fuck my asshole!" She could feel his fingers pulling out, the rubbery skin of her anus clinging to them and making a sucking, hissing noise as her sphincter reluctantly released them. Then she felt him push the cheeks apart again and she cringed forward, grinding her breasts down into the sandy bottom of the aquarium. Any second she expected his bluntly throbbing cock to ram into her back passage, but to her surprise, she felt his hot breath raking the crevice between her ass-cheeks, his tongue flicking teasingly at the tortured opening. His mouth clamped tightly over the hole next and his tongue thrust through, forcing a low, guttural moan from her throat. The sensation aroused her to new heights of passion, and she squirmed maddeningly before him.

"Oh God. Go ahead. Stick it in. Go ahead!" she begged. "Hurry before I go insane!"

As she wailed this cry from her lust-wrenched lips, he withdrew his mouth and moved his body up tight between the backs of her thighs, making her quiver with anticipation. She felt the mushroom-like head of his cock resting in the split between her buttocks, quivering as though ready to go into action any second. Supporting herself with one hand, she reached back between her legs with the other and cupped his heavy balls in her palm.

"Damn, she really does want it," she could hear the teenage boy's excited voice.

"Come on, Catherine, baby, get the Mayor's cock in the right place," the police chief bellowed.

Catherine's hand moved hesitantly from his lead-like balls and fear shot through her as she perceived how long it was. It was even longer than the contractor's, though not quite as thick. And it was going inside her ass. God, she was really going to be split apart this time. She stroked it tentatively, trying to decide what to do.

"Stick it in that hole, Catherine," the Mayor urged her. "Stick it in that hot little ass of yours."

Her fingers trembling, she submitted to the Mayor's command, holding her breath as she placed the quivering tip against her hairless opening. Feeling him begin to probe forward, she realised that her fears had been real, and that she had let herself be taken away by the heat of passion. It would never fit. Oh God, it would wreck her insides. His hips and knees wriggled around as he began working it slowly inside her, the head throbbing and making her asshole jerk wider. The pressure against the tiny opening was unbearable and something had to give way.

Her rear muscles strained and suddenly there was a popping noise followed by a spasm of excruciating pain that made her twist her face down in the sand, her red tresses flying over her back from shoulder to shoulder as she did so. Her buttocks moved back savagely, her belly and back undulating like a crawling snake. Her jerking, bucking motions sank the rod of flesh behind her deeper and deeper into her anus until she was moaning and screaming like a banshee. The men watched with lewd grins on their faces as she tried to escape by jerking forward, but the Mayor's hands were dug tight into her hips, and he was holding her locked to his loins.

"Awwwghhh!" she groaned from the pain, her face twisted and contorted from the ravishment of her virginal anus. "It's t-tooo big!" she cried.

The Mayor merely grinned and shoved into her without pity.

"Start moving that ass back! Move it in circles!" he barked, as though he were giving orders to an assistant.

Her eyes burned with tears of confusion and she could hardly think. There was no way to escape the brutal pain that was being inflicted on her by the Mayor's long, pulsating cock ramming into her asshole, threatening to rip her inner organs asunder.

"Come on, girl, push back," the police chief whooped from beside her.

Suddenly she clenched her eyes tightly shut, gritted her teeth against the pain and did exactly as she was commanded, moving her buttocks back against the long, bulging cock ramming into her back passage.

"Oh! Oh! Oh!" she chanted madly as the

monstrous shaft slowly burrowed deeper into her belly. She jerked forward quickly, unable to go through with it, but he was right up against her without wasting a second.

With a quick forward flick of the hips, he buried his cock practically to the hilt in the soft, flaccid tunnel of her ass. The pain seared through her belly, and she fought savagely for a full minute longer against the brutal skewering until with a final groan she ceased her struggle.

Rattling gasps heaving from his chest, the Mayor began sawing rhythmically into her deep back passage, burying his rampaging instrument to the balls in her skewered rectum with each excruciatingly brutal forward thrust.

Then, before the unbelieving eyes of the crowd, Catherine began grinding her hips backwards, rotating them in wide circles as she revelled in the cruel sodomising of her ass. The grinning Mayor slammed into her with hard, pitiless thrusts, his lips bared back over his teeth, his nostrils flaring as he sucked in huge gasps of air. His face was contorted in a mask of delight as he stretched the pink flesh of her ass on the out-stroke and then drove it back in hard on the in-stroke.

Catherine wagged her head from side to side, all the muscles in her body straining, the veins in her neck standing out in high relief as her face reddened, and she crooned and wailed in the incomprehensible language of lust. Her hair tangled wildly around her face as her buttocks jerked and belly undulated. As the cock rammed into her, her body was flooded with spasms of masochistic joy that gave her a strange, delightful pleasure. She wallowed obscenely in the lewd ass-fucking, raising and lowering her hips, driving them back and forth like powerful pistons. She gasped in pleasure as his testicles smacked rhythmically against her cunt below, sending quivers of excitement through her loins. Behind her she heard the hard-driving Mayor groaning and grunting each time he jerked into her, bringing moans and mewls from her own throat as he did so. She waved the whiteness of her ass back at him, desperate for him to shoot his sperm deep into her back passage.

"Ohhh! Ahhh!" she groaned and gasped as he pressed forward as hard as he could, pulling her ass-cheeks wide apart to allow him to sink deeper. With one hand she reached back under her body and cradled his balls again, scraping her nails over them in a maddening, teasing motion that brought saliva drivelling down over her back.

"Goddamn, she's movin' that ass!" the police chief gasped appreciatively from off to the side, as he stroked his hardened cock in lustful appreciation.

Suddenly she felt another movement around her head and a pair of knees sinking into the sand in front of her. It was the teenage boy, the contractor's son, and he was gripping her temples tightly, forcing her head upward. Her gaze came level with the youth's stiff, quivering cock that looked as though it was going to explode any minute.

"Damn, suck me!" he begged. "Y-ya gotta suck me!"

Quickly his thumbs were on her lips, prising them apart and forcing her mouth open. Before she even had a chance to think, his white, youthful cock had slipped in between her teeth.

"Oh yeah, oh yeah!" he groaned, throwing his head back. "Look, Pop, she's suckin' me."

God, she hoped Jefferson was watching all this. She no longer cared about herself but about humiliating him, about punishing him for what he'd done to her.

"You baaaastard!" she screamed mindlessly, hoping that he could hear her outside the tank.

From behind her, the Mayor gave a monstrous effort, sinking his shaft even deeper in her rectum until she jumped forward from the sudden pain. Her face ran head on into the cock poised between her lips and it suddenly went deep inside her throat. She could feel its stiff pulsations against the insides of her cheeks, tiny droplets of pre-cum already seeping down her throat. She could feel his hips twitching as he fucked into her viciously, anxious to spew his youthful load of sperm down her throat. Catherine gagged as his cock rammed halfway down her throat, the full length of it disappearing between her lips until only the very base remained protruding from the nest of his wiry pubic hair. She struggled for breath, her nostrils flaring, her face growing red. She could feel hot churnings of lust inside the fleshy instrument buried in her mouth and wondered if he was going to cum inside her throat. He quickened his thrusts to match those of the Mayor fucking into her ravaged asshole, never quite pulling it all the way out but leaving a slight part of the tip beyond her lips in the hot, moist shelter of her mouth.

There was some deep instinct inside her, which made her appreciate what was happening on a basic animal level. The desire inside her belly flickered again and, as the mental picture of being skewered by two cocks from different ends danced through her mind, the desire began to flare up like a raging fire. She rolled her buttocks high up behind her in a pulsating circular movement, tightening her sphincter muscles around the hot staff of flesh impaled beneath them. She wanted to milk it dry, to fill her belly again with torrents of hot male sperm, until the sticky fluids ran out of her asshole and trickled maddeningly down the insides of her thighs.

Her cheeks puffing and hollowing, she began to suck fervently on the throbbing cock buried in her mouth, her tongue swirling wildly over and around the blood-filled head, feeling it twitch and throb inside her throat. She wanted the horny teenager to cum inside her throat now.

God, how she wanted it!

It was the first time she'd ever tasted a cock, and she explored it hungrily, her tongue flicking at the blood-filled head, slowly gliding into the tiny slit at the end of the tip. She wanted it to shoot in her mouth, to swallow and feel it pouring down her throat to meet the sperm that would soon be shooting into her entrails from behind. She wanted it to run through her body in great, gushing torrents.

Behind her the Mayor was fast building toward his climax, bucking into her harder and faster in a wild frenzy, battering his hips mercilessly against the quivering cheeks of her ass with a leathery smacking sound.

His hands gripped her tiny waist, his fingernails digging deep into the soft flesh, bringing a cry of resistance from her throat that was immediately muffled by the cock buried deep in her mouth. She moaned incessantly at the dual ravishment of her loins as the teenager reached down underneath her and began squeezing her breasts in a frantically building rhythm. His eyes were aglow with savage delight, and he threw his head back as she sucked hungrily on his bulbously pulsating cock.

The Mayor prised her ass-cheeks as wide apart as they could go, smacking into her with resounding thuds as sweat dripped from his face onto her undulating back, and his breath rattled in his throat with the effort of keeping up with her madly pistoning body.

Catherine worked with dazed passion, licking and sucking crazily at the youthful cock skewering her mouth. Her saliva began to grow sticky as a tiny emission dribbled from its tip, leaving a pungent, salty taste that she swallowed hungrily, her Adam's apple bobbing up and down in a tense, quick rhythm. The boy's hips were jerking and straining below her bobbing head, his fingers tightly tangled in her long, red tresses, pulling the hair at the roots in his mad desperation to reach orgasm.

Suddenly as her loins spasmed inwardly, Catherine felt the cock in her mouth stretching and expanding until it made her cheeks puff up with air. She moaned and mewled and swallowed, sucking it in until it brushed against her tonsils, as though she were trying to make it join with the blunt instrument screwing into the depths of her asshole from the other end.

The boy's muscles suddenly stiffened as if his body had been charged by an electrical current, and he jerked his hips tight against her face, the full length of his cock burying itself in the depths of her constricted throat.

"Awww, yeah, I'm gonna come!" he wailed, his eyes rolling up toward the ceiling.

Desperately, Catherine sought to breathe through her flaring nostrils, wheezing and gasping and nearly choking on the boy's expanded cock flesh that grew and pulsed inside her mouth. Suddenly, his sperm rocketed forward in quick, sharp jets, flooding the depths of her throat as her cheeks filled with air, and her Adam's apple bobbed madly up and down. She sucked and swallowed with crazed gulps, but still fountains of white, creamy sperm poured out between her lips and dribbled down her chin, dripping slowly into the sand. The boy fell backward, overcome by the ecstasy. His cock was still joined to her lips by tiny, thin strands of cum, but she licked them clean, hungry for every ounce of salty, male fluid that she could swallow.

With the teenager lying in front of her, she arched her back low and waved her buttocks high in the air, screwing them feverishly back on the great, plunging cock that threatened to rip out her insides. She felt it throb suddenly and knew this could mean only one thing.

Her thighs and buttocks were swept wide apart in one last crushing lunge as the Mayor shoved the full throbbing length of his cock into her wide-stretched rectum, jerking convulsively, his hands tearing at her flesh like the talons of an enraged eagle. Catherine screamed muttering, guttural groans, her lips moving and mouth working as incoherent grunts poured from her body. Suddenly with a jerk, the Mayor's cock began spraying hot jets of sperm deep into her anal passage.

"Oooh!" She shrieked out her release as his orgasm flooded her body like a gigantic tidal wave. She screwed her buttocks back against the frenziedly jerking cock, feeling her body explode into a thousand shards as it ripped up inside her. His cum backed up and seeped around his cock, spewing down the backs of her legs in free-flowing rivulets as she ground and writhed, her teeth gnashing, her fingers clawing madly at the sand. One, two, three, the jerks of his cock came until finally it was all over, and he withdrew the deflated organ from the crevice of her ass with a popping, hissing sound. Immediately she fell forward, her arms sliding out until her belly and breasts crushed against the

182 ★ Kurt Robard

sandy bottom of the tank. In her state of sated exhaustion she thought she could hear gasps and murmurs coming from somewhere outside the aquarium, but only when she turned her head toward the glass wall on the outside could she see that a crowd had gathered and that they were eyeing her with amazement. Her body froze as she realised she was the centre of their attention, and then she quickly closed her eyes.

Where was Jefferson, she wondered, as the ecstatic experience of what she'd done had begun to wear off, leaving her with only shame and humiliation. She needed him desperately; she had to find him. Groping for her clothes which had been scattered about, she collected them and hurried toward the door leading out from the aquarium tank, immediately receiving the answer to the question she had posed inwardly, for Jefferson was standing right in the doorway.

She fought back the tears as she approached him.

"Jefferson, I'm sorry. I wanted to teach you a lesson. I didn't know it would be like this."

But immediately, she could see that his attitude hadn't changed at all. He was looking at her with a frozen stare on his face.

"I can't hear a word you're saying," he

spat bitterly at her. "As far as I'm concerned, we're finished."

"Jefferson, please. I want you."

He laughed hollowly and sneered at her.

"Want me? What for? I've only got one cock to fuck you with."

"Jefferson, please!"

But it was no use. She could see that he wanted nothing to do with her. He had merely come to humiliate her one last time, as though she hadn't been humiliated enough in one evening. And giving her one last look of disdain, he turned away and left her sobbing naked in the doorway.

Chapter 9

Catherine had never imagined things could be so bad between her and Jefferson. They had hardly spoken in the days following that night, and when he looked at her it was as if he was burning with hatred and disgust. She was hurt that it could have come to this, but she too was angry. It seemed so wrong that he could blame her so entirely for this mess, and she could not give in to the injustice of it. After all, it had been because of his infidelity that the whole thing had started in the beginning.

As for her, despite their problems, she felt liberated and womanly. She hadn't had sex since that night, and she was aching with a need to be fucked again. When Jefferson left in the morning and she had the place to herself, she stretched out over the bed, touching herself and bringing herself to climax again and again. She felt insatiable and desperately hungry for a big cock inside her rather than her slender fingers, and she repeatedly played over the sensation of being fucked by a group of men in front of an audience, moaning and thrashing on the bed.

Catherine was feeling more and more desperate and her relationship with Jefferson felt doomed. The night before, he'd managed to spend less than five minutes in the same room with her, and had exploded in anger at her attempts to bring them back together. While she masturbated, her memories of that fateful night were intermingled with his hateful, stinging words of that argument.

"Well, it's all over now. Our marriage is finished, and my career is ruined," he had yelled at her, throbbing with anger. "If you had only given me what I wanted, instead of that puritanical, pathetic line." Again, he had slammed out of the house, only to return early in the morning, exhausted and drunk.

By the end of the following week,

Catherine had begun to realise that only one thing could bring Jefferson and her back together. She had to show him how sexy she was, how great a fuck she was and, more importantly, how she was his and how much she loved him.

* * *

Jefferson had found it impossible to work that week. He had gone through the motions, working long hours in his lonely laboratory, avoiding the canteen or social areas, arriving before others did and leaving after they left. He played over the scenes again and again in his mind. His Catherine being fucked by the Centre's director in the boardroom, begging to have it harder and faster. His wife, being fucked up the ass while she sucked off a teenager's cock in front of all those people. He still could not quite believe it.

The thoughts turned him on, but they quickly turned to disgust at her betrayal and her dishonesty. He could hardly even look at her. Every night that week he had picked up a different girl in a bar or a club, and taken her home to vent his frustration and his hurt on their sweet little pussies. Then in the day, he would get out his cock at his desk and rub it hard and fast, moaning out loud until he came, gushing all over his leather seat.

Jennifer had dropped by once, and he had let her kneel down beneath his knees under his desk and suck him off, thrusting himself in her small mouth mercilessly until his release.

By Friday, he was exhausted and confused. He arrived early in work again, but by lunchtime had achieved very little. He stepped out of the lab for ten minutes to get some air and some lunch, stealing around the corridors hoping to avoid Dr Marlingham or Jennifer, or indeed any of the others who were present that night. He returned to the lab via the prep room, where his two young assistants were mixing up chemicals to aid Jefferson in his work. The back wall of the prep room contained a window which looked through into Jefferson's lab. He chucked the unwanted limp sandwich into the industrial bin and passed through into the lab, which was gloomy from the rain-soaked clouds outside.

As he entered the lab, he saw a shapely form bending over one of the lab tables. Her white lab coat was tightly fitted to her curves, and when he looked down to her legs, all he could see were fishnet stockings leading to a pair of red stilettos. Hearing him enter, she turned to face him. It was Catherine.

Jefferson was shocked. She hadn't been to work since that night, and she certainly hadn't been anywhere near his lab. He felt his anger flare and began to think of putting it into words.

Pre-empting his anger and his remonstrations, Catherine put her finger to her bright red, luscious lips and gestured to him to sit down on his leather armchair. He hesitated. He wanted to shout at her again, to force her to leave what had become his refuge. But, as his thoughts came crashing in, he slowly began to notice the clothes and the attitude that she was wearing. Her lab coat was short, almost as short as her miniskirt, and it was tightly buttoned to just below her cleavage, where it seemed to burst open under her breasts, which looked beautiful, firm and proud. She wasn't wearing a bra, and the stockings seemed to be unimpeded by any skirt.

There was a long silence, whilst the couple stared at each other.

"I thought I'd show you what I am," she murmured. "And that I'm yours."

Jefferson took a sudden intake of breath as he saw her beauty again for what seemed just the first time. She slowly undid the three buttons on her coat and slid it off to drop on the floor, her body radiating a sex appeal he had never felt before. Her stockings and suspender belt were the only garments left on her.

Catherine lent back on the bench and

started to touch herself, from her neck to her breasts to her inner thighs and then to her pussy. He could see a soft gleam there – she was already wet. As she touched herself, she moved seductively, slight moans emanating from those vivid lips, and turned her back to him to lean over on the bench and expose her beautiful ass and the pink lips of her now-dripping vagina.

Jefferson felt himself respond to the image before him. She was an incredibly beautiful woman, and his anger with her was beginning to subside. His cock started to throb gently in his pants as her finger began to move more quickly in and out of her vagina. He began to lose awareness of where he was. She turned to face him again.

"Get your cock out, and touch me with it," she whispered in a low voice. She could see his mood change and become receptive to her advances. Out of the corner of her eye, she saw movement in the back room but dismissed it as the rapidly changing light creating moving shadows on the walls.

Jefferson unzipped his pants, let his hardening cock fall out, and started to massage it in time with her own movements. He heard a movement behind him, but his tiredness and change in mood left that thought undisturbed. He was rapidly getting excited, and his cock was engorging by the second. He couldn't take his eyes off her; she was moaning loudly now, and brought her hand to those lips to suck and lick at her own juices whilst with her eyes she demanded more from him.

"You can do anything you want to me."

Jefferson had forgotten their dispute; all he wanted to do was fuck her hard in every way possible. She seemed different, changed, and she seemed truly sexy and wild. He stood up and stripped off all his clothes, but remained a distance away from her for a little longer, watching her revel in her new-found sexuality and lust.

Catherine had become aware that behind Jefferson, his two lab assistants were standing in the window of the prep room, watching the couple with excited expressions. They could not keep their eyes off her in her abandoned nakedness, and their voyeurism excited her still more, until her juices were all over her fingers and dripping on the floor. As Jefferson stared at her breasts and her pussy, she stared directly at the two assistants with suggestive eyes, and she saw them both reach down and undo their trousers.

Jefferson moved over to her and without a word, he lifted her up on the bench to lie down on her back. Her legs were slightly spread and her pink, engorged pussy was exposed to the three men. Jefferson bent down and began to tease and pull at the lips with his mouth.

"Spread your legs," Jefferson demanded.

Following his command, Catherine lay flat on her back, her legs spread slightly apart, her arms outstretched. Falling to his knees, he gripped the backs of her thighs and levered them upward, bending forward to clamp his mouth over her vagina. He began a slow nibbling motion with his tongue amidst the warm juice, and then his tongue began spearing in between the tiny dilating lips at a quicker tempo, bringing a subdued groan from her throat. Jefferson flicked his tongue against his wife's tiny clitoris until her thighs ground against the bench and she began breathing heavily.

"Ummmh, like that, Jefferson. Oh yes, suck me!"

She spread her legs still wider giving him greater access to her cunt, and for the first time could feel genuine charges of pleasure pulsing through her belly. His face was tight against her, his tongue flicking like a racing lizard inside her, bringing back all the memories of the things the men had done to her at the party. She was surprised to find how fast she was growing horny, when before it would have taken almost hours to get her to this state. She understood now that since this had all happened, she would no longer believe in that prudish morality.

She looked to the prep room where the assistants had been watching, and saw that they had moved out and were standing in the doorway to the lab, their two cocks throbbing violently as they watched the act enfolding before their eyes. The beautiful redheaded woman was wild, moaning and begging for more and more. Not conscious of anyone apart from the horny couple in the lab, they began to moan too as they strained to get a better view. They could not believe that such a thing was taking place, and wondered who this woman could be, hoping to be next in line.

"Deeper, deeper, stick your tongue in deeper," she begged her husband. Her head tilted back, and she clenched her eyes tightly shut, her white teeth glistening as her lips bared back over them. He dropped his hand to massage his cock, which was now throbbing with pain for the lust he felt for her. Her pussy was so sweet and it was contracting furiously around his tongue.

"Stick your cock in me now!" she screamed. "I need it. Oh God, how I need it!"

Jefferson's eyes rose to admire the gorgeous woman splayed out on the bench. He became aware then of his two assistants who had come closer to the couple to get a better view. He hesitated briefly, but as Catherine moaned at the decrease in pressure, he returned to her, proud to let them watch this amazing woman be fucked by her husband. He was sure now that she wasn't going to resist him or give him any kind of lecture on morality. For the first time in a long while he was really going to enjoy having sex with her.

"You'll get it, my darling. Right now!" Jefferson responded to her. Jefferson stood up to let the tip of his cock rest against the opening to her pussy. He enjoyed that moment as he stood, poised, to take his wife and fuck her senseless, and as he did so, he heard one of the assistants climax in anticipation, moaning and spilling his cum over the floor.

He rammed his cock into Catherine's cunt, her wetness letting him slip straight in and right up the length of her vagina. He screamed in pleasure, her pussy contracting around his throbbing penis and he felt its heat coursing through his veins. She clamped her legs tightly around his buttocks, and dug her heels into his ass-cheeks to spur him on, all the while a litany of other-worldly groans coming from her throat. Jefferson's buttocks flexed and hollowed, his powerful arms supporting himself against the bench, his feet planted solidly apart on the floor which was becoming stickier and stickier by the minute. His head was bobbing back and forth as he thrust rhythmically into her, groaning and snorting in time with the second assistant, who had lost all sense of himself and was reaching his climax.

Catherine's belly and hips bucked and jerked with each animal-like thrust of Jefferson's cock into her pussy. Damn, she really had become a whore, and all this nonsense about her never repeating what had happened at the party was just so much bull. The incredible thing was that his anger had completely disappeared and he was suddenly overcome with a powerful desire to do lewd, obscene things to her. She felt so alive, and her next seductive glance at the assistant sent him throbbing into a moaning orgasm.

Jefferson watched Catherine as she defeated the second assistant, and was all his. He felt his cum boiling up his penis with every contraction of her tight pussy. Screaming through gritted teeth, she suddenly spread her legs wide, raising them high in the air so that her feet pointed upward at the ceiling. Gasping and writhing, her body jerking in mad, spasmodic palpitations, she began to come, and with her, Jefferson above her let out a loud groan that sounded almost like a death rattle. His cock jerked and twitched, his hips slammed madly up against Catherine's pussy, and they came, loudly and simultaneously.

Jefferson collapsed into her arms, their love juices mingling together and seeping out of her pussy. Jefferson's penis lost its hardness and he rested his head awhile on her breasts; both were panting and exhilarated.

"It's about time we did it like this," he said to her gently.

Catherine smiled naughtily.

"And it's about time I did this," she murmured.

For a moment her eyes danced teasingly at him, and then she gripped his hard male flesh, slowly running her fingers up and down over the foreskin, and he felt himself filling with desire again, desire for his own wife to suck him off like he had always wanted.

"Suck me, sweetheart," he commanded. "Suck me now."

"Oooh! How could you ask me to do such an obscene thing?" she laughed and, repositioning herself on the bench, slowly slipped her head down and swirled her tongue out around his cock as he moaned in blissful satisfaction.

Their problems were over now, she thought. They would be able to have enjoyable sex whenever they wanted with each other, and when they got bored they were always free to go to one of the club meetings. It was a damned good idea I had to apply for that job, she thought, and then she began to concentrate fully on satisfying her husband. He was never going to be frustrated again.

He wasn't at the moment, either. A tickling sensation was travelling up the flesh of his body, beginning at the toes of his feet. A light, almost spidery touch wafted over his skin. It was her tongue, and every atom in his body was alerted, every inch of him throbbing with newly found desire. Her tongue was like velvet...

Just a few of our many titles for sale...

Lazonby's Heiress

Little does Alison realise her duties as secretary of Lazonby Hall include being a sexual 'play-doll' for the lascivious desires of all in the house. Mrs. Simpson is Mistress of the Hall in name, but now it's Alison's luscious young body that holds the title!

Helen's Southern Comfort

In the heat of the night Danny watches as his innocent wife is treated to pleasures she has never experienced before by his well-endowed neighbour. So begins a journey of sexual discovery for the Nielson's that takes them to the very edges of extreme sexual practices.

EVELINE

Gorgeous nymphet Eveline embarks on a dizzying path of sexual encounters as she tries to satiate her urgent needs on as many men as possible. Vania Zouravliov's rich and vibrant drawings bring explicit life to this unparalleled story of teenage debauchery

GAMIANI

One of the most important novels to have come off the 19th-century presses, this novel explores one night's abandon by the Countess Gamiani, her lesbian lover and a voyeur turned protagonist. Shockingly explicit, even by today's standards.

Eros and Thanatos

A high-art treatment of hardcore subject matter, this book contains the stunning work of late artist Klaus Böttger. Sex is lovingly, graphically depicted as bodies writhe at the very pinnacle of ecstasy. Contains two short novellas.

The Lost Drawings of Tom Poulton

British erotic institution Tom Poulton completes our trilogy of his work with this set of drawings that were previously thought to be lost. Also contains one of the dirtiest short stories, illustrated by the artist, the EPS has ever published.

The Secret Art of Tom Poulton

The first in the series of Tom Poulton books, this is a must for any erotic library. Containing some very graphic illustrations from this master of his craft it shows Poulton at his orgiastic best. Also contains two period novellas.